P9-ECR-828

SKODEN
vince
Uncle Bobby
JADA
CUZZINS FOR LIFE!
MUSQUA
Navajo

Kohkom & Moshôm
Dez and Rheana
Mom
Dad is Rad

Groundwood Books is grateful for the opportunity to share stories and make books on the Traditional Territory of many Nations, including the Anishinabeg, the Wendat and the Haudenosaunee. It is also the Treaty Lands of the Mississaugas of the Credit. In partnership with Indigenous writers, illustrators, editors and translators, we commit to publishing stories that reflect the experiences of Indigenous Peoples. For more about our work and values, visit us at groundwoodbooks.com.

MAGGIE LOU, FIREFOX

MAGGIE LOU, FIREFOX

ARNOLDA DUFOUR BOWES

ILLUSTRATIONS BY

KARLENE HARVEY

GROUNDWOOD BOOKS
HOUSE OF ANANSI PRESS
TORONTO / BERKELEY

Published in 2023 by Groundwood Books / House of Anansi Press
groundwoodbooks.com

We gratefully acknowledge for their financial support of our publishing program the Canada Council for the Arts, the Ontario Arts Council and the Government of Canada.

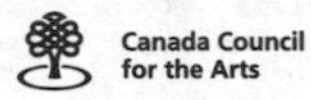

Conseil des Arts
du Canada

With the participation of the Government of Canada
Avec la participation du gouvernement du Canada | Canada

Library and Archives Canada Cataloguing in Publication

Title: Maggie Lou, Firefox / Arnolda Dufour Bowes ; illustrations by Karlene Harvey.
Names: Dufour Bowes, Arnolda, author. | Harvey, Karlene, illustrator.
Identifiers: Canadiana (print) 20230135307 | Canadiana (ebook) 20230135366 | ISBN 9781773068817 (softcover) | ISBN 9781773068824 (EPUB)
Classification: LCC PS8607.U3643 M43 2023 | DDC jC813/.6—dc23

Jacket illustration by Karlene Harvey
Design by Lucia Kim

Printed and bound in Canada

Groundwood Books is a Global Certified Accessible™ (GCA by Benetech) publisher. An ebook version of this book that meets stringent accessibility standards is available to students and readers with print disabilities.

Groundwood Books is committed to protecting our natural environment. This book is made of material from well-managed FSC®-certified forests, recycled materials and other controlled sources.

Maggie Lou, Firefox is in memory of our mom, the Queen Bee, Louise Marguerite Dufour "Calon" (1941–2022). Thank you for teaching me to stand strong and never back down.

This book is dedicated to all the Maggie Lous in this world who are living wild adventures in their imaginations — in their backyards, or around the world. Especially to my beautiful and amazing daughters, Rhiannon and Keana; and stepdaughters, Nikki and Jahda.

"Boxer in a Tutu" is in memory of Michelle Nelson (1978–2021), professional bantamweight Canadian champion, a dear friend and boxing coach.

"A Girl and Her Hammer" is in memory of our dad, Arnold Dufour (1940–2022), who taught me all I know about construction, and so much more.

"Prairiewalker, Sister of Bushwalker" is dedicated to the strong men in my life — my husband, Jeff; son, Josh; my brother Vince; hunting friend Bob; and stepsons, Shelton and Chad.

Moshôm
Kohkom
Uncle Bobby
ME!!
MUSQUA
DEZ
RHEANA

Mom
Dad
Vince
JAYDA
Navajo

ONE

BOXER IN A TUTU

1

ONE OF THE MOST BRILLIANT ideas I've had yet happens while I'm making a cheese sandwich. I hate cold cheese sandwiches, so I melt them in the microwave. I love sinking my teeth into the warm gooey cheese.

While I'm waiting for the cheese to melt, the microwave bell rings. It makes me think of the bell that rings between rounds during the boxing matches I watch on TV with my moshôm.

We are big boxing and wrestling fans at my house. On Saturday mornings we all sit around with our bowls of cereal and watch these crazy wrestling matches on TV. We cheer on our favorite wrestlers like Death Stare, the Dragon Wagon or Johnny the Knucklehead and laugh our heads off as they throw one another against the ropes.

So when that microwave bell goes off, it's like a lightbulb goes on in my head. I snatch my cheese sandwich from the microwave and run into the living room at full speed, tossing it between my hands like a hot potato.

I come to a sudden halt in front of the TV. I lick the cheese off my arm, then hold the sandwich above my mouth and let the melted cheese drip onto my tongue. This is my favorite part of cheese sandwiches.

Dez is lying on the floor staring at the television, moving his head back and forth trying to see around me.

"Guys! I have the most brilliant idea!" I yell.

Rheana's lying on the couch reading a teen magazine. She thinks reading this stuff makes her older.

She looks over the edge of the magazine and rolls her eyes.

"Not again," she says.

Dez raises his eyebrows. "How brilliant?"

"Westling!" I mumble through a mouth full of gooey cheese. "Wet's westle!"

Dez jumps to his feet and hunches over like a bear with his arms reaching out toward me like giant claws.

Scrunching up his face, he glares at me through his eyebrows and sways back and forth.

"I'm in. Let's goooo!" he yells.

"Good grief." Rheana turns a page.

I grab a pillow from the end of the couch and throw it at her.

"Come on, you fun-sucker!" The pillow hits her magazine, sending it flying into her face.

"My magazine! You're gonna tear it!" she screams. She sits up and throws the pillow to the floor.

Then out of nowhere, Dez tackles me from the side. We go crashing onto the couch, landing on top of Rheana. My sandwich goes flying, and our dogs, Navajo and Musqua, chase after it.

"Oh, my gosh, you guys are such losers!" Rheana yells, trying to push me off while I'm struggling with our annoying brother, with his knee on my chest and a mouthful of my curly hair in his mouth.

"Not yet!" I'm yelling at Dez.

"Get off me!" Rheana pulls her legs from under

me, plants her feet against my back and sends Dez and me onto the floor with one giant heave.

Landing on top of Dez, I quickly pin his arms down.

"Not yet!" I scream.

"When!" he yells, flipping me to the side as he sits up.

"After we build a wrestling ring!"

"Woo-hoo! How?"

SMACK!

A pillow hits Dez in the back of the head.

"You tore my magazine, you brat." Rheana waves the torn pages above her head.

Dez is about to pounce on her when I dive between them. Pushing them apart, I hold a hand on each of their chests.

"Hey, hey, hey. Let's keep this clean, kids." I look back and forth at them. "Let's settle this WWE style."

Staring at each other like two angry tigers in a cage, they circle one another and nod, both preparing to pounce.

VRRRRROOOM.

We look out the window and see Mom's car pulling into the driveway.

"WWE style. Tomorrow." I hold out my hand.

"Tomorrow," Dez says, placing his hand on top of mine.

"Yeah, okay, whatever." Rheana puts her hand on top of ours.

"TOMORROW!" I shout.

Dez returns to the floor and stares at the TV. Rheana plops down on the couch and flips through the torn pages of her magazine.

I go down the hall to my room. What will be my signature move? A backwards flip? A clothesline across the chest and finish them off with an elbow to the stomach? Or the famous suplex, where I grab Dez from behind, bridge backwards and toss him over my shoulder onto his back?

So many choices for a girl to make.

And how to design a wrestling ring and not destroy any of Mom's furniture? Do we even need bouncing ropes?

The good news is, I am very creative.

According to my teachers, I'm "a determined

leader, courageously brave and firm in my beliefs," even though some of my classmates say I'm just bossy and stubborn. But my mom always tells me, "Keep taking up space, Maggie. You're only making room for the girls behind you."

But sometimes stuff happens when I'm being creative. Like when I made a spacecraft using cardboard, bubble-wrap and duct tape. When I couldn't convince Dez to get in, I put on a bike helmet and oven mitts for safety gear and went barreling down the stairs. I just didn't consider how my rocket ship would come to a stop at the bottom.

Mom had to wrap a tensor bandage around my ankle. She doesn't find my accidents as exciting as I do.

Thank goodness she's a nurse and has nerves of steel.

My mom says my wild ideas come from my dad's French side of the family, while my dad insists my stubbornness comes from my mom's Scottish roots. But they both agree that my adventure-seeking nature comes from my Cree and Sioux side. They say it's in my blood, that it runs in the family.

I'm lying on my top bunk, drawing designs for

a wrestling ring, when I hear Mom and Dad walk into the kitchen.

"Come and help with groceries!"

I jump down, and all three of us kids run out to the car and place as many bags as we can on each of our arms. It's kind of a competition to show who's the strongest. I like to take the lightest bags and leave the heaviest ones for Dez.

As we unload the bags on the kitchen table, Mom eyes us up and down slowly.

"Why are you all so quiet?"

She looks around the room suspiciously. Dad unpacks food into the fridge.

"And you all jumped to the pump as soon as I called?"

Mom continues to look around and moves to the living room.

"What were you kids up to today?"

"NOTHING," we answer.

Mom and Dad stop and stare at one another. All three of us smile at the same time.

"Why would you think we were up to anything?" I say.

Mom continues to look around the living room, then bends down behind the couch. Slowly she holds up a half-eaten piece of my cheese sandwich in one hand and, in the other, a handful of crumpled pages from Rheana's magazine.

"Oh. Gee. I don't know, Maggie. Why would I ever think that?"

2

"AAAAANNNNNDD . . ." I'm standing at the window finishing my blueberry muffin. "They're gone!"

As soon as Dad and Mom have pulled out of the driveway the next morning, we move the couch, loveseat and chairs into a kind of square to make a wrestling ring. We remove all the breakable items and move the coffee table and end tables outside the ring so we don't wreck them.

Navajo and Musqua want in on the action, and they start nipping and chasing one another around me as I'm carrying a lamp to the hallway, nearly making me drop it.

"Bad dogs!"

They bow their heads and look up at me all sad.

Putting the lamp in the closet, I turn and rub their soft fuzzy heads.

"But you're both still cute."

Navajo is a German shepherd. He's smart but sometimes gets into trouble because he's so active and doesn't always make the best decisions. He was a runt and starving when the rescue shelter found him in a shoebox on the side of the road. But they nursed him back to health. He's been on the go ever since and can be annoying, but I love him. He reminds me of someone I know!

Musqua is a chubby border collie whose name means bear in Michif. He reminds me of my sister Rheana because he's lazy and loves to sleep.

We make a padded floor with blankets, in case one of us tries to suplex the other. The dogs once again try to get in on the action by having a tug-of-war with the blankets. Dez finally puts them outside.

In no time our ring is ready for action, and so are we!

I stand in the center of the ring. Dez and Rheana are in opposite corners, glaring at each other just like a real wrestling match.

"In this corner, we have Dez Troy, the little maniac from the deep west side of Westside. Weighing in at a whopping seventy-eight pounds, with three wins and twenty-six losses," I yell, pointing in his direction.

"Twenty-six losses?" he shouts.

"Never mind, you're not the announcer." I continue. "And in this corner . . ." I sweep my arm across the ring. "We have the sucker of fun, crusher of dreams and most boring of bores." She rolls her eyes at me. "Weighing in at ninety-five pounds, with zero wins and nothing but losses . . . Ray Ray!"

I tilt my head back, cup my hands around my mouth and make crowd-cheering noises.

"Wrestlers, center." I wave them forward on either side of me. I place a hand on each of their shoulders. "Okay, wrestlers, we want a clean fight. No pinching, biting, scratching, hair pulling and nothing below the belt."

They nod.

"To your corners!" I push them away. Jumping over the back of the couch, I dash to the kitchen. Setting the microwave timer for two minutes, I hit the Start button and hurtle back over the couch. "Are you ready to rrruuummmbbble?"

But they are already circling each other in the ring. Dez shoots in for a two-legged takedown, but Rheana slides to the side and jumps on his back. Dez grabs at her arms, trying to remove our screaming sister from his back. She has her arms wrapped around his neck and her legs snaked around his waist like some alien parasite.

I wince. "Oh, no." I know what he's going to do.

Dez grabs her legs in one quick jerk, tucks his chin into his chest and flings himself backward onto the couch.

BAM!

"OOF!" They land on the couch with Dez's full weight on top of Rheana, knocking the wind out of her, but she doesn't let go.

Dez scrambles to pull himself from Rheana's python grip. As he squirms to turn around and face her, I wince again.

"Uh-oh."

Rheana quickly pulls her legs in, planting her feet in the center of his chest.

Suddenly, she lets go of his neck as she explodes her legs skyward.

For a moment, Dez is balanced on the soles of her feet as she thrusts them to the ceiling. His eyes pop open wide as saucers as he's lifted into the air.

Rheana then launches him off her feet with a quick flick, and Dez is briefly airborne until he hits the blanket-lined floor.

BOOM! OOF!

Rheana rushes to stand on top of the back of the couch. She stares down at our brother.

He slowly gets to his knees and turns to look up just in time to see Rheana jump from the top of the couch.

"KOWABUNGA!" she screeches, flying through the air.

She catches him with a Flying Clothesline and lands beside him with a loud crash. I run around the edges of the ring, pulling the blankets back into place so no one gets hurt.

The microwave bell rings.

"I'm out!" Rheana runs to restart the microwave.

I jump to my corner, excited to be next. Dez

crawls on his knees and uses the couch to help himself up.

"Give me a min . . ." he chokes out.

"AND FIGHT!" Rheana yells.

I run toward Dez, not giving him a moment to think. He looks up just in time to brace himself. Our heads tuck into opposite shoulders as I tackle him in what my dad calls "right to the numbers," which means driving my shoulder straight into his chest.

We go soaring back into a chair. It slides on the hardwood floor, making a loud scratching noise.

"That's gonna make a mark," I wheeze out in between breaths.

The chair rocks back and forth, almost flipping as we come to a stop. Dez attempts to use Rheana's flying push-kick move, but I feel his legs reaching under my belly and back away.

As he lies back in the chair, I quickly grab his ankles, yanking him to the ground.

THUD!

His back hits the hard floor.

"Ohh!" I hear Rheana gasp from the sidelines.

Dez moans. I drag him to the middle of our ring,

pulling the blankets along with him.

He catches his breath and starts to squirm and kick. Releasing his ankles, I prepare to launch an attack from the side, but he turns his body to keep his feet facing me no matter which way I scramble. I try to push them to the side, but he's too quick.

Finally, I see my perfect opening. I dive in, scoop both legs underneath his knees and pull them back over his head. I fold him over into what we call the Crusher.

Pressing his knees to the floor to one side of his head, I lay on all my weight.

Then suddenly, he lets out a giant FART!

PPPFFFFFSSSSSTTTTT!

It's like a giant wet explosion in his pants.

"BAHAWHAWHAW!" Rheana falls over laughing.

I release his legs, instantly gagging from the smell.

"Oh, my gosh, DEZ! What did you eat? A death burger?" Holding my nose, I crawl away.

Dez roars, "Oh, just wait! There's more!" He scuttles toward me.

"Oh, dear sweet cheese of Switzerland, NO!"

I rush to stand up, but not quickly enough. Dez jumps on my back like he's riding a horse.

"Giddyup!" he yells as he lets another fart rip.

"AGGHHHH! Get off me, you disgusting kid!" I yell, struggling to remove him.

He wraps his legs around my waist and arms around my neck. Rheana is rolling around the couch laughing so hard I'm sure she's going to pee her pants.

"Not until you say I'm the champion!" Dez yells in my ear as he hangs on for dear life.

"Not a chance, stinkmeister!" I try to stand up with him attached to me like a backpack.

PFFFFFFFTTTT!

"You asked for it, Dez!"

I reach behind me to grab the back of his neck with both hands. Then I flip my head toward the ground, and Dez flies over my back into the chair.

The chair slides … "OOOOFFFF!" Dez whispers as he lies upside down in the chair.

"Okay. Enough of up close and personal. Let's do this the old-fashioned way!" I say, walking into the kitchen. "I have another brilliant idea."

"I hope the old-fashioned way is less smelly!"

Rheana gasps, still laughing. They follow me into the kitchen.

Grabbing Rheana's hands, I thrust a pair of Mom's flowered oven mitts onto them.

"Cool!" Dez says. "A bake-off."

"No, Sir Fartsalot." I wrap tea towels around the mitts. "Boxing!" I secure the large mounds on her hands with shoelaces pulled from Dad's work boots.

"Voilà!" I hold up her hands. "Boxing gloves!"

"Great, but what about my perfect smile, Maggie?" Rheana scrunches up her face and bares her pearly whites at me.

"I have an idea!" Dez raises his eyebrows up and down a few times, then digs around in the cupboard. He unrolls a sheet of paper towel and tears it in half. Wadding it up, he sticks it in his mouth and chews, transforming it into a pasty mess, then presses it to fit around his teeth.

"In … tan … out … ard," he mumbles.

"What?" Rheana shakes her giant mitts at him.

"IN … TAN … OUT … ARD!"

I shove the other half of the paper towel into her mouth.

"Chew it up, Rheana. It's gonna be your mouthguard."

"Ohhhhhh." She starts chewing.

I find another pair of oven mitts for Dez, pink with white polka dots. I wrap them in yellow checkered tea towels and tie them with laces pulled from Mom's running shoes.

We march back to the wrestling ring. I toss the blankets over the back of the couch, as we no longer need a padded base.

"Boxers! Take your corners!" I yell from the middle of the ring.

"In the red corner, we have Dez PowerFart O'Malley!" Dez pumps his fists in the air and lets out a small fart.

PFFT.

Shaking my head, I continue, "And in the blue corner, we have Whinesalot Sissypants Rheana!"

She rolls her eyes at me.

"Okay, boxers. Keep it clean and make it quick. Mom and Dad will be home soon!"

I leap over the couch to the microwave, and as I hit start, I yell, "BOX!"

* * *

"What's with the new furniture arrangement, Maggie?" Mom asks as she walks around inspecting the living room.

She stops at the end table in the corner and notices there's a different lamp on it. Then her eye moves up the wall to a noticeable hole that we made when Dez jumped from the end table to nail me in the gut with a flying elbow, and the table slammed into the wall.

She shoots me That Look, moves the lamp and places a yellow sticky note with *Fix Me* written on it above the hole.

We are then ordered to vacuum, mop and dust the entire living room.

We have just finishing cleaning when Dad arrives home from work. He walks into the house, takes one look at us cleaning and immediately spots the sticky note.

"If I wanted holes in my walls and doors knocked off, I should have had a house full of boys!" he says, shaking his head.

But he winks at me as he goes to get his toolbox.

Dez hits me in the back of the head with a cushion off the sofa.

"Yeah, ya should have been a boy, Maggie Lou!" Dropping the pillow, he takes off down the hall.

"Well, maybe you should try being a boy sometime instead of a baby!" I yell, picking up the pillow and chasing him as he runs to his bedroom.

I continue pushing against the door, and Dez pushes back, keeping it closed.

"Dad! Make her stop!" Dez yells from behind the door.

"Dad, make her stop . . ." I mimic him in a whiny voice and start banging hard on the door with my fist. It's a battle of wills and maybe a little payback for that flying elbow he threw at me earlier.

"DAD!" he calls out louder.

"MAGGIE LOU!" Mom shouts from the kitchen.

"DEZ!" Dad yells from the living room.

"WHAT?" we both scream.

"Take it outside," Dad sighs.

Suddenly the bedroom door flies open, and Dez rips past me at full speed. I'm immediately on his tail, pillow still in hand.

Rheana casually opens the front door and whispers, "Gosh, you two are annoying," as we roar past her into the front yard.

"Elvis! That's not helping," yells Mom.

"Well, at least they can't break anything outside," Dad says, laughing.

I scramble to toss Dez to the ground.

"*Tân'si,* Maggie Lou!" I hear Moshôm from behind us. "*Tân'si,* Dez."

I am holding Dez down by the scruff of his shirt with one hand, pillow in the other.

"Hi, Moshôm."

Moshôm and Kohkom are walking up the sidewalk, Kohkom carrying fresh bannock wrapped in a tea towel. It smells wonderful.

"You're not fighting again, are you?" Kohkom asks, shuffling past us.

"No, just having a little sibling fun!" I call out, pinning Dez's shoulders down while I lean over him.

"Good. Cause I'd hate to see one of you get hurt," Moshôm says as he helps Kohkom climb the front steps. Dez sticks his tongue out at me, and I let a string of spit drool from my mouth and hang above his face.

"MOSHÔM! MAKE HER STOP!" Dez cries out. I hold him down harder and laugh like a crazed villain.

"Maggie Lou," Moshôm states firmly.

I quickly suck the string of spit back into my mouth, let go of Dez and stand up.

Mom, Dad and Rheana are all standing on the front porch.

"Sorry," I answer, ashamed, as Dez stands up and sticks his tongue out at me again.

"You should be." Moshôm laughs. "That's not how you fight."

"Yeah! That's not how you fight!" Dez smacks me over the head with Mom's pillow, drops it, then runs around the cedar trees with me in pursuit again.

"Boxing is the only true form of skilled fighting," Moshôm continues as I zoom past the steps.

"That girl has too much fire for her own good," Moshôm says as he helps Kohkom climb the last step.

As we round the cedar trees a second time, I grab the back of Dez's T-shirt, and with my other hand reach for the pillow and smash it into his back with all my might.

It breaks open. Feathers are flying everywhere!

Moshôm laughs, "Firefox!"

"My pillow!" Mom yells.

Everyone on the front porch is laughing except Mom. Her hands are on her hips, and she doesn't look amused. Dez and I are covered head to toe in feathers.

"More like Fire Chicken," Kohkom pipes up.

3

A FEW DAYS LATER, Moshôm arrives for another visit.

"Hey, Fire Chicken. I mean Firefox." He chuckles and sits beside me at the kitchen table. "My girl, do you like boxing?"

My eyes light up as I look up from my cheese sandwich.

"YES, Moshôm!" I lean in closer, hoping to hear the words I've been waiting for.

Moshôm was a boxer when he was young, and now he works as a boxing coach with boys at the Friendship Centre.

"Good," he says, and gets up to make more tea.

He stands at the counter stirring sugar into his tea, then looks at me.

"You'll come with me tomorrow to the Friendship

Centre. I'll teach you to box."

I drop my sandwich and leap out of my chair like a racehorse out of a starting gate. I run to Moshôm, almost knocking him over as I wrap my arms around him.

"Thank you, Moshôm! Thank you!"

He messes up my curls and laughs.

I disappear into a daydream about dancing in the ring. My entry song, "Fire Woman" by the Cult, plays in the background as I walk up the aisle toward the boxing ring in a sparkling black robe. Moshôm walks proudly beside me. My head is down and I'm deep in thought, getting my mind into the match. The bedazzled black hood is draped over my head, and a beautiful fox is engulfed in flames on the back. As I swing my winning combos in front of me, it looks like she's dancing in the fire.

That night I lie awake for hours, tossing and turning so often that I get tangled in my bedsheets. I lie in bed dreaming of entering the ring to the sound of people cheering, seeing my mom, kohkom and aunties screaming in the crowd.

I must have fallen asleep at some point, because my tired eyes pop wide open as the first rays of sunshine leak through our bedroom curtains.

I leap down from the top bunk, not caring how much noise I make.

Mornings are the worst time for my hair. It bounces around my head like a lion's mane when I land.

Rheana screams from the bottom bunk.

"Nothing to worry about, little sis." I dance around the room, punching the air. "That's until I learn how to BOX!"

She lies in her bunk, glaring at me.

"Go away. You're annoying," she says.

"You just wait, Rheana. I'm gonna float like a boat and sing like a bee." I throw a few fast punches in combination. "BAM BAM BAM!"

Rheana rolls her eyes. "It's float like a *butterfly* and *sting* like a bee. Oh, my gosh!" She pulls her blanket over her head.

I ignore her. She's annoying and is only eleven, which means she knows nothing. Besides, I am busy finding the perfect outfit to wear today. I'm so excited about being in a real boxing ring, and I need to be ready!

I dig through our dresser drawers, tossing shirts, shorts, pants, socks and underwear onto the floor until our room looks like a clothing explosion went off.

"Ah-ha! Found it!" I hold up my pink bodysuit. It has been my favorite since Halloween, when I dressed up as Black-Eyed Ballerina, my own original wrestler character.

On the front is a picture of a boxing kitty-cat, and around the waist there's a sparkling tutu. I pull it over top of a pair of black leggings and toss my pajamas onto Rheana's bed.

I bounce into the kitchen. My mom is still wearing her nursing uniform because she just got home from a night shift.

"Wow! Morning, Maggie Lou. You look amazing." She kisses me on the forehead and sits down at the table. "So, what adventure are you on today?" she asks, taking a mouthful of cereal.

"I'm going boxing with Moshôm! He's going to teach me today!"

Mom nearly chokes. She spits cereal across the

table, and bits of it land on Dad's face. He is reading the news on his phone.

"WHAT?" Mom yells.

Dad looks up, pieces of cereal clinging to his cheeks.

"Yes, dear. He asked to help with her . . . energetic nature. Besides, if she's busy in the ring, maybe the shenanigans here will stop," he continues calmly, wiping his face with a napkin.

"Seriously? And he offered!" Mom slams her bowl down as she gets up from the table. She marches straight to the phone. "All my life I asked that man to teach me to box. But he refused to show me how to throw a decent punch!"

Mom picks up the cordless phone and furiously punches the keys.

"And you know what he told me?" She stares at Dad. "He told me the ring is no place for a girl!"

She stops to point the phone at Dad. "And now! NOW he decides to teach HER!" Mom continues to hammer Moshôm's number into the phone.

I think she may break it.

"Well, honey," he says calmly, "times have

changed. Besides, you should be happy. Maybe she'll stop taking chunks out of the living-room wall."

Mom rolls her eyes at Dad like Rheana does so often at me and turns her attention back to the receiver in her hand.

"Yeah. Morning, Dad! What the heck?! You're teaching Maggie Lou to box?" she bellows. "I asked you for years as a kid, and you always said —"

Suddenly she looks down and goes quiet. "Uh-huh. Yeah."

She turns her back to us.

"Yes, Dad. Uh-huh." She continues to listen to whatever Moshôm is saying on the other end.

They hold a quiet conversation in Michif for a few moments.

"Okay," she finally says. "Fine. But you'll have to teach the other two as well. They'll need to protect themselves. She is a bit much at times."

I am a little insulted but too excited to care.

She turns back to us, still talking to Moshôm. "Yeah. I know where she gets it." Glancing my way, she winks. "Okay. Yes, love you, too. See you later."

She hangs up and glares at Dad.

"I still think you're the one behind this, Elvis."

I get up and quietly pour a bowl of cereal.

"Well? What did he say to calm you down?" Dad asks.

Mom sighs. "He said he was afraid."

"Oh, really?"

As I return to the table, I accidentally spill milk on the kitchen floor. I wipe some of it with my sock foot, then quietly sit down, careful not to interrupt their conversation.

"He said I was just as wild as Maggie Lou, but he was afraid I'd hurt someone."

I look at Mom, confused. She would never hurt anyone. She's a nurse, and she helps everyone she knows.

"He was afraid I'd hurt myself." She laughs. "I was a little accident-prone as a kid and didn't listen well." She joins us at the table. "He reminded me that when I was eight, I tied pillows to the trees in our yard and pretended they were punching bags. That's how I broke my hand."

She shows us the scar where she had screws put in. "I missed the pillow."

We all laugh.

"Besides, it *is* a different time. Back then, there weren't any women boxers," Dad says.

Mom looks at me and smiles. "True. And Moshôm's right. That's why he named her Iskotêw Mahkîsîs as a baby."

"Firefox," I whisper.

"And Dad reminded me of Michelle, their star female boxer. She's now the professional bantamweight Canadian champion. Boxing has changed for the better."

"Plus, Maggie Lou is a great listener," Dad says.

Mom stares down her nose at me. "And I guess you're right. It's better if she learns the correct way, or she *will* hurt herself."

Yes! I silently cheer to myself and jump up off my chair to kiss Mom on the cheek. She shakes her head at me, smiling.

As I run out of the kitchen, Dad lifts his hand for a high-five. I jump into the air and raise my hand to meet his, but instead, I slip on the milk I spilled, and my body hits the floor like a ton of bricks.

I lie on the kitchen floor in my sparkly tutu

staring up at the ceiling, slightly stunned.

"Like mother, like daughter!" Dad bellows.

All three of us explode with laughter.

4

AT 10 O'CLOCK DAD DRIVES me to the Friendship Centre.

I can't believe this day has arrived! My legs tremble and my heart flutters like a large butterfly inside my chest as we walk into the building.

As we step into the smelly gym, I feel my sparkly pink tutu bounce around me. At first I wrinkle my nose in disgust from the horrible stench. Then I think of all the older, experienced boxers who went before me, all the lessons and bouts they've done in this very gym. I hope those experiences will be transferred into my brain in some magical scientific way.

I lift my chin and suck the musty air into my nose.

All the boys stare at me as they pass us on their

way to the ring. I know they're staring at my tutu or wondering what I'm doing here, but I don't care.

As my mom likes to say, "Big hair, don't care."

Moshôm walks up to us, shakes Dad's hand, hugs me and welcomes me to the club. He introduces me to Coach Johnny and the boxers as Iskotêw Mahkîsîs, his little Firefox.

A boy about my age with splotchy cheeks and crooked teeth points at my tutu and laughs.

Moshôm shoots back at him, *"Pôn' wêwita!"* which is Michif for be quiet.

With Moshôm's arm around me, we walk to the back of the gym. I turn my head to the boy, sticking out my tongue at him.

"Okay, my girl. First rules of boxing. Respect the ring, the rules, the officials. And most of all, respect your trainers and opponents," Moshôm instructs me while he examines my hands. "Respect your body. Know your body. If it hurts, that's your body speaking to you. You have to speak back to it. You will need to listen to your body. It will tell you when to go on, when to push through and when to stop."

He grabs a handful of my hair and tries to tie it back the best he can, struggling to gather all of it with an elastic band.

I am so excited my hands are sweating. I still can't believe this is happening.

"That was your mom's problem. She could never listen." He laughs. "If you want to box, you need to know how to listen and follow directions." He lifts my chin and looks into my eyes. "Understood?"

I nod. All I can imagine is my big entry into the ring and my flashy satin black robe flowing behind me.

Moshôm walks into a small room off to the side of the gym.

When he returns, he smiles at me and places an old wooden-handled mop and a rusty metal pail sloshing with water in my hands. It smells like a swimming pool.

"Good. Now mop and dry the ring."

Then he walks away.

The smile painted on my face all morning just melts into a frown.

"But when do my boxing lessons start?" I call out.

He keeps walking toward the boys who are wrapping their hands and yells back, "They already have."

All the boys laugh, and I feel my face go red.

I mutter to myself as I mop the dirty canvas.

"If I wanted to do chores ... I could have just stayed at home ... Maggie Lou do this ... Maggie Lou do that. Geesh! I should have stayed in bed!"

But I remember a couple of important lessons drilled into me during my twelve years. Respect my Elders, and do a job well the first time.

So I do what Moshôm has asked.

After I finish mopping, I dry the ring with a towel that's wrapped on the end of a push broom and held in place with wide elastic bands.

Standing in the corner of the ring, I watch the boys warming up on the floor. Some are doing drills on punching bags, while a few practice using hand pads. Some of the boxers approach the ring wearing headgear and gloves.

"Glad we have a sparkly maid here now!" says the crooked-toothed boy through his mouthguard. "Can you get me a water, doll?" He laughs as he walks past me.

Moshôm is behind him and smacks him lightly on the back of his headgear.

"Mikey, that's enough! *Hâ mâka*, hurry up! Your kohkom moves faster than you!"

I laugh as I leave the ring carrying the mop and pail so the boxers can spar.

I spend the next month cleaning the ring every Saturday while wearing my sparkling tutu. After the boxers spar, I disinfect their smelly gloves and headgear, hand-wash their hand wraps, hang them to dry and sweep the gym floor.

Every week I ask Moshôm when my boxing lessons will begin.

He always says the same thing. "They already have."

Some days, I have to carry the blue plastic pail labeled with a black marker as the Spit Bucket from the corner of the ring to the bathroom to be emptied. I try not to retch and am careful not to stare too deeply at what is sloshing inside the pail. The splattering noises when I empty it are bad enough. I walk straight to the bathroom with the bucket, flush it quickly, rinse, dump and rinse again. Then I scrub my hands with tons of soap and hot water like I'm a surgeon preparing to operate. But really, I'm just trying to wash away the disgusting thought of the bucket.

I'm starting to question Moshôm saying that my lessons have begun. I don't understand how all this cleaning has anything to do with boxing! But I keep doing the jobs he gives me, hoping there's a purpose behind them.

I hold the ends of the broom and mop handles like giant chopsticks and use them to pick up yellow sweat-stained towels and hand wraps that reek like zombie feet. I carry them to the laundry room with my giant chopsticks and toss them into the washing machine. I dump in extra scoops of laundry soap for good measure to kill the wretched smell wafting up from inside the washer.

Actually, I dump in a LOT of extra soap!

A short while later, Mikey leans into the equipment room where I'm sweeping.

"Hey, Sparkles! Something's wrong with your washing machine!"

I stop and listen. I hear loud swooshing noises from the next room.

Dropping the broom, I run to the laundry room, nearly knocking Mikey over.

He follows me, and we stand at the door with eyes bulging like basketballs. The entire room is filled with bubbles that pour out from beneath the washing-machine lid like foamy white lava!

Bubbles are everywhere!

"Well, at least we know the wraps are clean," Mikey says, smacking me on the back before he walks away.

Moshôm appears carrying a small white bucket and two large empty yogurt containers. Placing them in my hands, he sniffs the air.

"I love the smell of freshly washed laundry."

I spend the rest of the morning using the yogurt containers to scoop mounds of soap bubbles from the washing machine, and the small white bucket to remove all the bubbles from the laundry-room floor.

Covered in bubbles from head to tutu, I carry the containers to the bathroom and dump them into the shower stalls and toilets.

It's a lesson I'll never forget. More soap doesn't mean more clean!

***

Every Saturday, I struggle with the giant metal pail that smells like an over-chlorinated swimming pool. Moshôm has taught me how to carefully mix the bleach-to-water solution in a strong enough ratio to kill the boys' stinky germs, but not so strong it will wreck the equipment.

As I mop the floors near the heavy bags, I hear Moshôm call, "Iskotêw Mahkîsîs, get me my first-aid bag."

I run to his office, grab his red duffel bag and carry it to him.

On the bench at the edge of the gym, he is inspecting Mikey's feet. Moshôm examines them, then digs around in his red bag.

"Feels like my foot is on fire, and it's so itchy," Mikey moans.

"You should try showering." I scrunch my nose and look down at his feet. "They look like two hairless mole rats with a weird rash. EWWWW."

Mikey squints at me. "I'm probably allergic to you!"

I stick my tongue out at him.

"*Scrime*! Both of you, it's athlete's foot." Moshôm applies ointment on Mikey's feet and hands him a tube, instructing him to take it home.

"Well." I pick my mop back up. "At least there's one thing athletic about you, 'cause it's not in the ring."

Mikey whips his infected sock at my head. I quickly duck to avoid it and stick my tongue out at him again.

Moshôm shakes his head as he gets up and explains, "There's a lot of sweaty people in and out of here. This is why everything needs to be cleaned well."

"Yeah! Do your job, Sparkly Maid!" Mikey hollers.

"Yeah! Well! You just keep your feet clean, Fire Foot!" I yell back as I continue to mop.

The entire gym bursts into laughter, and I realize everyone has been listening to us.

"Fire Foot and Firefox!" one of the boys bellows.

Moshôm rings the bell. "Okay, back to training!" He walks over to me.

"Full of pee and vinegar, I always said." He laughs

as he takes the old mop and rusty pail out of my hands. I shake my head because I still don't understand what that means.

Holding my hands, he massages them and announces, "I think today is a good day, Iskotêw Mahkîsîs."

Then to my amazement, he begins to wrap my small hands in the wraps I have grown used to washing.

I stand there, watching him zigzag, loop and turn the fabric around and around my hands.

FINALLY, my day has come!

When Moshôm finishes wrapping my hands, he carefully marks the concrete floor with a letter X in chalk. He explains where to place my feet as I move around the chalk lines, how to position my shoulders and hands and how to distribute and shift my weight.

For the next several Saturdays, he has me practice moving forward, back and side to side around the X marked on the floor.

I get bored doing these exercises. I want so badly to jump into the ring. I want to hit someone.

But I repeat, "Listen, Maggie Lou, listen. First rules — respect and listen."

It has been eight Saturdays, and I haven't even hit a bag!

I've mopped, swept, wiped, jumped rope and moved my feet around — back and forth, up and down, over and around.

Then Moshôm has me practice dipping and moving under and around ropes he has strung around the gym, but I never get to punch anything.

Soon I don't even have to look down at the chalk marks on the floor anymore. I start to dip and weave around the ropes without thinking.

I wonder if I'll ever learn to box.

"Cleanup on aisle eight!" Mikey calls.

I look up to see Moshôm and Coach Johnny in the boxing ring, waving for me to grab the mop and pail. Blaine, one of the older boxers, is bent over in the middle of the ring, holding his nose as it drips blood all over the canvas.

Maybe I should have taken up wrestling instead, I think as I head to the ring, dragging the mop behind me.

5

IT'S ANOTHER WEEKEND IN THE smelly gym.

I walk through the door with my gym bag in hand and my sparkly tutu bouncing around me.

The wet smells of sweat and bleach no longer hit me like a brick wall. My nose has become used to the smells of the gym. It is still full of teenage boys' feet and body odor, but all I smell is the boxing ring now.

I move the wraps and towels from the washer to the dryer as soon as I arrive. They are from extra training with the competitive boxers on Friday night.

As I leave the laundry room, I notice that someone has written on the soap box in bold black letters: ONLY 1 SCOOP OF SOAP PER WASH!

I laugh as I remember all the bubbles that filled that small room. What a funny day that was!

Tossing my bag on one of the wooden benches that line the wall, I plop down and squeeze my feet into the blue-and-white boxing boots Moshôm bought me a few weeks ago. They look like high-top runners but have soft leather bottoms, and they fit differently than regular runners.

Moshôm says they should fit like a glove and feel like nothing on my feet, because I'm supposed to feel the mat of the ring under me. I mostly feel strange wearing them because I don't like how they look. I'd rather wear my white runners with pink laces that I got at Christmas. But Moshôm says if I'm going to be a boxer, I should start looking like one.

Still, I draw the line at my tutu, which I'm not going to change any time soon.

"Hey, Sparkly Maid! Wanna come mop up Sam's defeat?" Mikey yells from the ring. "It's in the ring, along with his dignity!"

Laughing, Mikey smacks Sam on the back as they crawl under the ropes.

Mikey is so annoying. Like my little brother but worse.

Mikey and Sam make their way to the bench.

"What's on the agenda today, Sparkles?" Mikey asks as he removes his gloves.

Sam sits down, holding a water bottle awkwardly with his gloves, taking long sloppy swigs. Sweat drips down his face from beneath his headgear, making a large wet spot down the front of his shirt.

Boys can be so gross!

I throw a towel at Sam.

"Oh, you know," I tell Mikey. "Same old, same old. A little of this, a little of that." I stand up to leave. "And a whole lot of everything else."

"You mean a whole lot of nothing and more cleaning!" Mikey laughs loudly, removing his headgear. His black hair is sopping wet and sticks to his large skull. He looks like a drowned rat.

"Unlike you, Mikey," I reply, "some of us listen and try to learn from our coaches." I grab the hand wraps from my bag. "And someone has to clean up after you filthy smelly animals!"

"Hey. We're not that bad," Sam says, water dripping from his lips.

"Besides, if it weren't for us, Sparkles, you'd have nothing to do but boring drills all day long."

Mikey stands up beside me. "We add a little spice to your training." He places his sweaty arm around my shoulders. A strong smell that reminds me of a raccoon that died under our outside steps last summer wafts up from his armpit.

"No, you add smell, Fire Foot. That's all you add." Pulling away from him, I shake my head in disgust and start to wrap my hands the way Moshôm has taught me. Over, under, around. I repeat this movement until my hands are wrapped and protected in my bright pink hand wraps.

"Smell. Spice. Whatever." Mikey laughs as he walks away. "You like us, Sparkles. Otherwise, you wouldn't keep coming back."

"Oh, my gosh! Are you serious? I come here for boxing, Mikey! Not smelly boys!"

"Which smelly boys?" Moshôm asks from behind me, laughing.

"Oh, sorry, Moshôm. I meant —"

"It's okay. They are very smelly." He hands me an elastic. As I tie my hair back, Moshôm tosses me a skipping rope and walks back to coach the boys in the ring.

I move to the side of the gym, still mad at Mikey. I do warm-up drills and my twelve minutes of skipping rope.

Moshôm says all great boxers skip. All I know is I never liked skipping during recess, and doing it with a bunch of smelly guys in a boxing gym is no different. I've counted four new whip marks on my shins from doing double-unders!

I get my ponytail caught in the rope while I'm speed-skipping, and Mikey has a good laugh.

"Sparkles! Maybe you should stick to the mop! The skipping rope might be too much for you!" he yells across the gym as I untangle myself and stick my tongue out at him.

As I hang up the skipping rope, I notice Moshôm whispering to Mikey. And as I walk to Moshôm to report for duty, I see Mikey in the corner starting a set of burpees.

I giggle, because we all hate burpees more than skipping.

"Done warm-up, Moshôm. Am I on drills or mopping next?" I ask.

He looks down at me from the side of the ring.

"I'm going to teach you something new today."

He steps down the small staircase and looks me in the eyes.

"Punches. We are going to learn how to throw a punch."

My heart leaps inside my chest. I am so excited as I think, *YES! My day has come!*

Then you know what happens?

My day still hasn't come.

Instead, I spend the next several weeks practicing. Not only moving along the lines drawn on the floor but also punching nothing.

Moshôm calls it shadowboxing. I throw jabs, double jabs, rights, hooks and uppercuts until my arms ache. I punch the air and am told over and over: "Extend your arm." "Turn your hand over." "Squish the bug!" "Use your hips." "Chin down. Hands up!" "Shoulder forward." "Turn your hip." "Use your body."

I'm getting SO tired of being told what to do.

I throw jabs, which are quick punches with my lead hand. They start and end at the side of the jaw. Cross or straight rights are exactly that, extending my right hand straight out. They are power punches because I use my entire body to torque into the punch, squishing an imaginary bug into the floor with my back foot while twisting my body and throwing the punch.

Standing at the gym mirror, I remember Moshôm's instructions for the uppercut. *Drive from the hip, don't pull your elbow back so much . . .* I hear his voice in my head.

I get into position and watch myself in the mirror, counting in my head and throwing punches in front of me: One, jab, two, straight right, three, hook and four, uppercut and . . .

WHAM!

I catch my own chin with my gloved hand, and my head pops backward.

"Quick hands, quick feet, Firefox for the knockout!" Mikey is laughing loudly, his mouth wide open. He looks like a hyena as he walks past me.

"Yeah. Well, quick mouth, slow brain, it's Fire Foot on the loose again!" I snap.

I keep practicing the endless punches in front of

the mirror without many more accidents. I start to throw the four basic punches like I've been doing them my whole life: jab, cross, hook, uppercut. Then I begin to move around and dip, roll and pivot with the punches.

Coach Johnny works with me sometimes and teaches me to throw what he calls combinations, but only in the air, again and again. And because it's not enough that I do these boring drills every Saturday morning, Moshôm has been picking me up to train on Wednesday nights. I practice them at home because even though the drills are boring, throwing punches is fun.

I even made my own heavy bag at home. I found an old foam mattress in the basement and a small aluminum culvert tube left over from Dad's last construction job. I rolled the mattress around it twice and tied it on using eight rolls of duct tape. I hope he didn't need them! I didn't know how to hang it in the garage but my cousin Jayda, who's excellent at construction, drilled three holes into the top of the culvert, attached a chain, then hung it from a hook on the garage ceiling.

Voilà! Instant heavy bag.

When Moshôm sees me practicing on my invention, he laughs, but he says it's funny only because it's so much like what my mom did as a kid when she tied pillows around a tree. He says the women in our family are innovative!

Some days at the gym, Moshôm holds hand pads in front of me as he calls out the combination number he wants me to throw. We move through the eight combos I've learned. I also practice blocking or moving by slipping, rolling or pivoting. We do fifteen to twenty minutes of hand pads. Then I do shadowboxing.

On other days he has me practice moving around the bag as I punch it, using all the combos he's taught me. Sometimes he holds the bag against his shoulder and yells out combos. Then he sends me to do more shadowboxing.

I want to hit someone in the ring like all the guys are doing.

But nope, Saturdays and Wednesdays it's me in front of a mirror, on the bag or punching hand pads.

It's so boring, some days I want to quit.

But no way am I going to quit in front of Fire Foot.

Mikey speaks up over the music as he passes me. "Come on, Sparkles. When you gonna give up and leave us?"

I ignore him and continue my drills.

"The only opponent you have is your shadow. And I think you're losing!" he snorts.

Not even thinking, I bend over, pick up a hand pad someone has left on the floor and hurl it so fast and straight like a missile, I even amaze myself. It lands squarely on the back of Mikey's sweaty head and makes a squishy noise before falling to the ground.

Mikey whips around to pick it up to return the shot.

"Firefox one, Fire Foot zero!" I hear Moshôm yell from the corner. He's leaning over the ropes of the ring staring at us.

I swear Moshôm sees and hears everything.

I put my head down and continue my drills in front of the mirror as Mikey slowly picks up the hand pad and returns it to the mat beside me.

"Quit while you're ahead," he whispers as he passes.

"Not a chance," I hiss back as I throw a combo number five in the air. "I'm just getting started."

6

EVERY TRAINING DAY is the same, whether it's Wednesday evening or Saturday morning.

Come in. Ignore the smell. Change my shoes. Skip rope. Shadowbox. Hit hand pads as Moshôm or Coach Johnny hold them or punch the bag. Then on to my list of endless chores.

I now join the boys for sit-ups and push-ups to end my days. I hate push-ups, but I am getting stronger. Now I can do them from my toes, not just from my knees. Some days I can do one more than Mikey. I like those days.

I continue to shadowbox in front of the mirror and daydream about how I can build a speedbag or a two-way bag to practice with in the garage.

I mostly bob, weave and throw punches to the

beat of the music that fills the gym. The older boys usually have heavy metal playing loudly. Most are fifteen and older and are competitive boxers. Some have traveled for boxing matches and have won medals and belts. It's great to watch them in the ring. The best of them seem to float on the mat like they've been doing this forever.

But they all talk about the best boxer from the club, Michelle. She's older now and lives in another province, running her own gym. They say she has legendary hands that move as fast as machine guns. I hope to meet and train with her one day!

BEEP!

Finally, my twelve minutes of shadowboxing are over. As usual, I walk to the closet and grab the mop and pail. Carefully following Moshôm's instructions, I mix the bleach-to-water ratio at the sink, then drag the mop and pail to the ring, wondering what ridiculous drill Moshôm will make me do today.

"My girl. *Âstam*," Moshôm calls out, standing by the doors of the gym. He and Coach Johnny are standing with Mikey and a new boy. The new boy stands confidently with a ratty pair of gloves hanging over his shoulders, a goofy grin, knobby knees and bushy eyebrows that look like giant caterpillars.

I push the mop and pail over to them.

"Yes, Moshôm?"

"This is Gary, Mikey's cousin. He's going to be joining us."

"Okay," I say. "Hi, Gary."

"Gary here is gonna be the best you've ever seen, Sparkles. One day he's gonna own his own gym, bigger than this place, and we will rule the boxing scene," Mikey brags as he puts his arm around Gary, smiling ear to ear.

"Well, best of luck. But you should find a different partner, Gary."

Moshôm shakes his head, "Give him the mop and pail. Coach Johnny will explain to him all that has to get done —"

But I've already pushed the pail in front of Gary and thrust the mop into his hand.

Gary's ear-to-ear smile disappears. His caterpillar eyebrows turn down.

With a mop and pail in hand, he follows Coach

Johnny toward the bathrooms and mouths quietly to Mikey, "What the heck?"

Mikey shrugs and walks to the ring.

Moshôm takes my hands in his. He looks into my eyes and says, "You'll spar today."

AHHHH! I want to scream!

My day has finally come!

As he leads the way to the ring, I notice Moshôm has a bit of a spring in his step. We arrive in the red corner, he wraps and pulls a pair of gloves on my hands and they feel magical. It's as though the heavens have opened up and shone a bright light down on me. I feel like a million bucks!

Then I realize.

I have to spar with Mikey.

He grins at me with his crooked teeth. He leans over and as he ducks under the ropes to climb into the ring, he whispers, "Okay, Sparkles, let's gooooo!"

I stand in the corner facing Moshôm. He can see my fear.

"Don't worry, Iskotêw Mahkîsîs," he says gently. "It's light sparring. You have headgear, a mouth-guard and light gloves on. Besides, you listen well.

Good listeners make the best boxers." He winks at me and spreads Vaseline on my face to protect it.

"Now, Mikey doesn't listen well. He needs a lesson." Moshôm shoves the mouthguard into my mouth, then turns me around to face the center of the ring.

Rubbing my shoulders, he leans in close and whispers, "He'll come straight at you. He always throws a high right hand and drops his left, leaving his face exposed. As I said, he doesn't listen well. I want you to keep your chin down and pivot as soon as he throws his right. He'll follow through in front and you'll see his chubby left cheek. Then plant a nice solid hit to his jaw. After that, just play around."

I listen carefully to Moshôm, but my heart is pounding so loudly I can barely hear him. He repeats his instructions and asks me if I understand.

I nod and take a deep breath.

Moshôm yells from the ropes, "Light, clean sparring, Mikey. You know the rules."

Mikey and I meet in the middle and touch gloves.

"Nice tutu, Frog!" he mumbles through his mouthguard.

I don't understand the frog reference, but I know it's an insult to my French heritage. My kohkom Rosa is from Montreal and speaks French.

And now this just got personal.

"Skoden," Mikey says, flicking his chin in the air at me.

"Stoodis," I mumble through my mouthguard, glaring into his beady little eyes.

We back up into our corners. I tuck my chin down, rocking my left shoulder forward as Coach Johnny has taught me, and my feet remember exactly where to go. My sparkly tutu jumps as I move in the boxer's bounce Moshôm made me practice over and over.

"You got this, Firefox," Moshôm whispers into my ear as he taps my shoulders.

The bell rings, and I feel Moshôm gently nudge me forward. I move toward the center of the ring.

"Light on your feet, keep moving," he calls from the ropes.

In my head, I repeat to myself, "Float like a bee. Sing like a butterfly."

And just then, Mikey does exactly what Moshôm

said he'd do. He doesn't bounce but just comes straight at me.

He charges toward me, mumbling through his mouthguard, "I'm Michael T. Kinequon from Gordon's First Nation Treaty Four. Prepare to feel my wrath, you sparkly tutu frog."

As Mikey moves toward me, I see him pull back his right hand high and drop his left hand away from his face.

I remember Moshôm's words and pivot. Then there it is! His chubby, splotchy brown cheek, just like Moshôm said.

And BAM! I let it go.

I throw a quick left jab, then a hard right, both landing squarely on the side of his jaw. Mikey turns toward me, but before he can do anything, I throw the combination punches that Moshôm calls from the side of the ring. My hands remember all those combinations he had me practice. I block a few of Mikey's jabs and avoid some of his straight rights. I slip his left jab, miss a hook and my head gets rocked with a quick uppercut, but I finish with a snappy jab, then a solid uppercut to Mikey's jaw that lands with a satisfying hard-squishy connection.

My heart is pounding loudly, and I'm out of breath. The 55-second event feels more like five minutes.

I back away, finally remembering to breathe. Mikey collapses to one knee. My mouth drops open. The entire gym is silent.

Mikey, now down on both knees, spits out his mouthguard along with some blood. Coach Johnny goes to help him, and the bell rings.

It sounds nothing like our microwave bell at home.

"HOLAY! Just deadly." Gary is standing ringside holding the mop.

I return to my corner, and Moshôm smiles as he takes my gloves off. I am breathless and amazed at what just happened.

"Well done, my little Iskotêw Mahkîsîs. I told you good listeners make the best boxers. So, what do you think of boxing?" he asks, his eyes twinkling.

I smile through my mouthguard. "I wuv it!"

"That's what I figured," he responds. "Just remember, it's not usually this quick or easy." He laughs. "This is only the beginning, and it stays in the ring."

I nod excitedly.

We walk down the stairs of the ring. Mikey, sitting on the side, hops down and shakes my hand.

"Well, Sparkles. You've earned my respect. Not only do you know how to clean the ring, but girl, you know how to throw some good hands."

I smile. "Thanks, Mikey T. Kinequon. Just don't call me frog again."

He nods. "Got it, Firefox."

Gary joins us, dragging the mop and pail behind him. "Maybe I should have you as a partner in my future boxing club."

Mikey chuckles as he removes his headgear. "Don't get carried away, cousin. She's a little much to handle."

"GARY!" Coach Johnny yells. "Bathroom!"

Gary frowns and runs back awkwardly, spilling water all over the floor with each step.

"Rookie!" I call out.

Mikey and I continue toward the bench.

"And no more bugging me about being a maid."

"Secret?" He leans in toward me.

"What?"

"All those chores your moshôm had you doing?"

"Yeah." I hold my breath, waiting for another one of his maid jokes.

"We all started there." He points with his thumb to Gary and the bathroom. "That's why I bugged you so much. Only the champs stick it out." He drapes an arm across my shoulders. "Or the stubborn ones."

We both burst out laughing.

"But now you need to tell me your secret. How did you learn so fast? I've been here longer than you." He stops and bends over to grab a water bottle from the cooler. "You must be really strong."

I lean far away from him. "Not as strong as the smell from your armpits!"

He turns his head to take a quick whiff and makes a face.

"You're not wrong there, Firefox!"

"My secret, Fire Foot? I just listen well. Maybe I could teach you," I reply as he throws me a water bottle.

"Deal! If you promise to keep the hitting inside the ring." He takes a big swig of his water.

"We'll see." I pour the icy water from my bottle over Mikey's head and bolt, racing across the gym.

TWO

A GIRL AND HER HAMMER

1

"SON OF A BILLYGOAT!" I drop my hammer and shove my throbbing thumb into my mouth.

Dez laughs like an evil clown at the accidental pounding I gave myself.

As he laughs, the half-sheet of plywood he's holding falls out of his hands and lands on his foot.

"Billygoat of a son!" he yells, grabbing his foot.

I watch him bounce around on one foot while I keep sucking on my thumb.

"What is going on back here?" Mom asks, peeking around the corner. She's been working in the flower bed that runs along the front of our house, and her face is sweaty.

"Nothing, Ma."

Dez plops down on the driveway, still holding his foot.

"Yeah, nothin', Ma. Just another one of Maggie's brilliant ideas!" he complains.

"Well, if you don't want to help her, I'm going to the greenhouse to grab some annuals, and I need help planting them." Mom turns on the garden hose. "So it's either help Maggie with her brilliant ideas or Mom with hers."

"Nah, I'm good, Mom." He hates shopping even more than our dad does.

Mom turns on the hose, rinses the dirt from her hands and wipes them on her work jeans.

"Well, I'm off. Maggie, watch the kids and don't do anything silly while I'm gone."

"When do I ever do anything silly?" I ask as I start nailing the sheet of plywood Dez dropped on his foot to the top of the ramp I'm building.

"Gee. I wonder?" she replies as she gets into her car.

As she backs out of the driveway, I scan the drawings in my favorite notebook. It's gold, with bold black letters across the front: *Plans to Dominate the World.*

Since Dad bought it for me last Christmas, I've filled it with ideas, plans and drawings. There are sketches of cardboard ships for sliding down stairwells, a tri-tire swing that would allow all three of us siblings to swing together, a treehouse built entirely out of scrap metal and duct tape, and a slackline to suspend over the above ground pool we got last summer. (That idea was quickly shut down as soon as Mom saw it.)

The edges of my book are getting tattered, but the camouflage duct tape I've used to repair it just gives it more character.

As summer holidays have begun and boxing is done until September, I've been keeping myself busy. Unlike my lazy sister, who binge-watches her favorite shows for days, I hate lying in front of the television. I prefer to be what I call courageously creative and busy as a bee.

I am currently building a ramp for my red Supercycle ten-speed. I have drawn a detailed 3D picture, complete with a list of the supplies I need to build it. My mom says lists are a woman's best friend.

Luckily, Dad has a large supply of wood scraps

that I can scavenge — pieces of lumber and plywood left over from various jobs. I knew I would need a lot of lumber, so I bribed Dez to help with a half-bag of stale Cheezies I found under my bunk bed and four partially melted mini-chocolate bars left over from last year's Halloween.

But as my dad says about my uncles who work for him, you get what you pay for! Because oh, my gosh, Dez is lazy! I have to keep an eye on him, or he disappears into thin air!

"Dez!" I look around for my helper. "Dez! We need one more piece of plywood, and then I can take this epic ramp for a spin!"

I finally spot him lying under the trampoline.

"DEZ! PLYWOOD! NOW!"

He crawls out of his hiding spot and sits up, orange cheese dust coating his lips and hands.

"Yeth, mathter," he mumbles through a mouthful of chewed-up cheezies.

As I begin to pull the massive ramp toward the middle of the driveway, I realize it's much heavier than it looks.

"Rheana! Come help!" I yell over my shoulder

toward the house as I try to drag the ramp by myself.

Rheana appears at the screen door. She leans casually against the doorframe slurping a purple popsicle.

"Yeah. What do ya want, bossy?"

She licks the popsicle from the top down and then follows a stream of purple juice with her tongue down her arm to her elbow.

"I need your help!"

"Please," she replies.

"Now!" I swear, if looks could kill, they'd be burning a death ray into my lazy sister's brain right now.

"Say please," she says, still leaning against the door.

"Oh, my gosh, Rheana! Now."

"No." She turns to leave.

"Fine! PLEASE."

My sister, who was apparently born solely to torment me, turns slowly, lips twisted in a goofy smirk. "With sugar on top."

"What?!" I shake my head and give up. I bend over and grab the ramp, preparing to move it alone.

Rheana opens the squeaky screen door and plops herself down on the steps. Taking the final bites of her popsicle, she watches me struggle. I pull, push and heave at it, but the ramp barely moves. I gather all my strength in one massive pull. My sweaty fingers slip and I tumble backwards, landing heavily on my behind.

Rheana giggles, purple juice running down the sides of her chin.

Still glaring at her, I spit out, "Please. With sugar on top."

Rheana wipes her lips and stands up.

"I thought you'd never ask."

Dez appears, dragging a ragged piece of plywood behind him.

"Drop it and help," I order.

He drops the piece of plywood. The three of us line up on the side of the bike ramp, then push it to the center of the driveway.

SCRRREEEEECCCCHHHHHH.

It makes the most horrible squealing noises as it scrapes across the cement.

"Right here!"

We stop pushing and step back to admire the chop-shop ramp I worked so hard to build. I grab the piece of plywood Dez dropped and hammer it into place over the one gap that remains on the ramp.

"PERFECTO!" I raise my hammer. "Why ride when you can fly!"

"Ummm. I don't know, Maggie." Rheana tilts her head, staring at the ramp. "It looks kind of . . . sketchy."

"You look kinda sketchy," I snap back as I run to the garage and grab my bike.

"I think it looks cool!" Dez runs up the ramp and jumps off the end. "I'm next!" he yells and grabs his BMX off the front lawn.

"Next to die," mumbles Rheana.

Ignoring her, I back up until the rear bike tire touches the garage door, lining up my ten-speed with the center of the ramp. I have to gather as much speed as possible before takeoff. I pull on my pink riding gloves and tighten the Velcro straps around my wrists. I flip my pink bicycle helmet with its spiky black mohawk onto my head and tuck as many curls as will fit underneath. I grip the handlebars, stand up on one pedal and stare down at the ramp.

I begin to rock back and forth and I yell, "Feel the rhythm … feel the vibe … come on, kids, it's go-go time!"

Pushing off with my back foot, I pedal like my life depends on it. I feel my curls whipping behind me like ocean waves.

I stand up, pushing faster and harder on the pedals.

I got this! I think as my front tire hits the ramp.

"NOPE! I don't got this," I mutter, my mind racing in dread as I hear a loud *CRACK!*

A board beneath me breaks, and instead of soaring into the sky like Evel Knievel, my Supercycle skids, and the front tire drops off the front end of the ramp.

I catapult over the handlebars headfirst. I hear my siblings gasp as my helmet hits the concrete and the plastic mohawk snaps off. I continue into a somersault with my bike still attached to me and land flat on my back with a loud moan.

I am painfully twisted up with my bent bike resting on top of me.

SQUEEEAAK.

The back wheel makes an annoying squealing noise as it continues to spin.

I cannot move.

Stunned, I stare at the blue sky with its fluffy white clouds floating past.

"BAWHAWHAW!" My sister cannot control herself and breaks out laughing loudly. Dez rides his bike up beside me, squealing his tires to a stop close to my head.

Rheana is still laughing as I slowly move my leg that's caught under the front wheel of my bike. I lift my head and notice the front rim now has a gentle curve that it didn't have before.

Dez stares at me and says coldly, "Move. So I can go now."

"Ohhh, you're in trouble. Here comes Mom!" Rheana exclaims.

SCCCREEEEEEECCCCCCCH.

Mom slams on the brakes as her car turns into our driveway. I'm lying in the middle of the pavement, crumpled up like yesterday's newspaper. I can barely move, and now I feel my leg burning.

"Maggie Lou! What did you do now?" Mom yells as she comes barreling out of the car. "Oh, my gosh!" She kneels beside me, staring at my leg.

I lie there silently, wondering why my leg feels like a small herd of red-hot elephants are trying to stampede out the side of it.

Shaking her head, she calls out, "Rheana, grab some towels! Oh, my goodness, Maggie! You cut yourself again."

I hear the screen door slam as Rheana runs inside. Dez keeps riding circles around us on the driveway.

Mom carefully untangles me and tosses my mangled bike aside. Rheana arrives with tea towels. I moan softly as Mom presses them firmly against my leg.

I'm trying not to make too big a deal out of this, but I'm glad she's a nurse.

"Well, at least you've had your tetanus shot." Mom continues to shake her head at me as she quickly examines the rest of my body. "Good thing you had your helmet, Maggie, or you'd be getting stitches in your skull . . . again!"

Helping me up from the cement, Mom continues, "If you hurt yourself one more time, I'm getting my sewing kit out and stitching you up myself!"

I lean on her as I limp toward the car at the end of the driveway.

"You know, if I weren't a nurse at the hospital, they'd be calling the police on us for the number of visits you make! Oh, my goodness, girl! What am I going to do with you?"

"Trade her in for a puppy!" yells out Dez, riding in circles around the ramp.

"Or a kitten! I like kittens!" shouts Rheana.

"You two, never mind! Walk down to your kohkom's house. She's home right now. We'll be back as soon as your sister is stitched up," she grumbles as I get into the back seat and press the tea towels to the side of my leg.

VRRRRROOOOM.

"Don't you dare bleed on my seats, Maggie Lou!" Mom warns over her shoulder.

* * *

"Well, if it ain't Evel Knievel!" Dad teases me the following day as I limp into the kitchen, clutching my *Plans to Dominate the World* notebook.

"More like his cousin, Crash and Burn Cathy!" Dez bursts out laughing between bites of toast and peanut butter.

"Hardy-har-har." I grab a bowl for my cereal.

"Ahh. Better luck next time, my girl." Dad sets his coffee cup in the sink and messes up my hair. "Besides, ten-speeds are not the ideal vehicle for catching air-time off a homemade ramp built from leftover scraps of plywood and two-by-fours."

"I blame my construction assistant!" I stare Dez down. "He was lazy on the job and gathered rotten old plywood." I pour cereal and milk into my bowl.

"Ya get what ya pay for!" Dez shouts, toast crumbs dropping from his mouth.

"You got that right." Dad stares up at the clock on the wall. "The crew is late again."

I gingerly sit down at the table, set my notebook next to my cereal bowl and wonder what I can do today.

Flipping slowly through the pages, I examine my

projects. It's summer break, and I gotta stay busy.

Dad finishes tying his work boots.

"Maggie Lou, whatever it is you're thinking of doing today," he says, "put it off until tomorrow. For your mother's sake."

"Or next week, Maggie." Mom appears from the hall in her fluffy pink housecoat. "Please. Give us a week. Your stitches need to mend anyway."

"It's fiiiiinnnnne, Mooooom," I call out, continuing to flip through my notebook.

"Maggie." She stares down her nose at me as she pours a cup of coffee. "A week."

"But what am I supposed to do!" I cry out, flopping back in the chair.

"You could take care of your dogs, Maggie," Dad says. He leans in to kiss Mom goodbye on the lips but scrunches up his nose and kisses her on the forehead instead. She rolls her eyes at him.

"I already put Navajo and Musqua outside. Remember to feed and water them." Dad opens the door to leave.

"Yeah, you wanted those beasts." Mom closes her eyes and takes a long sip of her coffee. "Maybe bathe them. They're beginning to smell again."

"That's a great idea!" Dad says as he shuts the door. "Okay. Later, fam-jam!"

I sigh at the thought of doing chores instead of going on adventures, but as I finish my cereal, my mind starts to whir.

Staring up at the ceiling, I notice a tiny spider spinning a web in the corner. I watch her weave her silk in and out, back and forth. She's so efficient.

Suddenly, the wheels in my brain start to turn faster!

I make checklists in my head — bathe the dogs, feed the dogs, water the dogs, play with the dogs . . .

How do I get this all done with one flip of a switch?

"Maggie. I hear those hamster wheels turning in your head. What are you concocting?" Mom asks.

"Nothing."

I grab my pencil crayons and ruler and head to my room to draw some of my ideas.

I can see it already. A wonderful doghouse.

No. A tower. A multi-level puppy tower.

No, even better. I will call it Caninetopia. A place

where dogs can have everything they've ever needed. A puppy spa-cation. A slice of doggie heaven here on earth.

As I reach my room, I hear Mom shout, "Next week! No doing anything but chores until next week!"

"Yes, Mom." And I shut my bedroom door.

Oh, my gosh. This will be the longest week of my life.

2

MY WEEK OF QUARANTINE IS UP, and I feel ten times better, like I could parachute off the roof of a skyscraper. I'm excited that two of the five stitches have dissolved, and my leg looks almost as good as new. I have had seven days of thinking, drawing, measuring and designing my brilliant new idea.

Caninetopia, a three-level dog mansion for Navajo and Musqua.

I have designed it so that each dog has his own bedroom — one on the second level and the other on the third. They will use ramps to reach their beds.

Unfortunately, Navajo has to wander through Musqua's room to get to his. But Musqua won't mind. He's so lazy that he won't even notice.

The main floor is their eating den, fully equipped

with a built-in water dispenser. I'm still working on how to get the hose and bowl to fill automatically so I don't have to spend time refilling them. Those dogs drink a lot of water during the summer.

My invention could be revolutionary for other dog people, too. I could make MILLIONS!

I sit on the back steps, turning the pages of my World Domination notebook as I figure out my plan of attack.

"Mornin' Maggie. What you destroying today?" My mom's brother Bobby laughs as he walks past me carrying an armload of tools.

I glare at him over my sunglasses. "I'm building a house. What are you pretending to be busy with today, Uncle Booby?"

He sets the tools in the bed of the crew truck. "Oh, you know. A little of this. A little of that. But mostly a whole lot of really hard stuff like breaking my back and working for a living."

He runs his hands through his thinning brown mullet.

"You mean drinking coffee and telling us what to do!" My cousin Jayda walks up to the truck and sets her toolbelt in its box. "Why are you lying to Maggie so early in the morning?"

Jayda is the first woman in our family to work construction. She's funny, wears long brown dreadlocks and has worked hard to become a crew manager. Dad says she's a quick learner, incredible at what she does, and he worries she'll leave to start her own company. That would mean losing his best worker.

I look up to Jayda. She's always encouraging me to try new things, to be brave and step out of the box. I'm not sure what box she's talking about, so I just keep trying new things and being brave.

"Don't listen to him, Maggie. The only hard thing he does all day is deciding whether to add one lump of sugar or two to his coffee," Jayda snorts.

"As if." Uncle Bobby walks back to the garage. "Jayda's lucky she knows which end of the hammer to use."

Jayda winks and whispers loudly to me, "Electricians are not real construction workers." She takes a big swig from her travel mug and peers over my shoulder. "What masterpiece you got going on today, Maggie?"

"It's Caninetopia," I announce proudly, pointing to the design in my notebook.

Jayda leans in closer, turns her dirty Blue Jays hat backwards and pulls back her dreads so she can see my plans more clearly.

"Hmmm . . ." She nods as she examines my plans. "Three levels, ramps, automatic water dispenser. Interesting." She nods again. "Is that a slide? And a pool?"

"Yeah. But I'm not sure how I'm going to work that in. My overall plan was to build a place they can eat, sleep, play and get clean, all in one building."

I turn the page to show her the plans I've drawn for each floor in greater detail.

"Their food and water are on the main floor," I point out. "Musqua's bedroom is on the second floor with a small mirror on the wall because that dog is conceited and loves to stare at himself. He reminds me of my sister."

Jayda laughs.

"Navajo's room is on the third floor and has a built-in shelf for his toys. He's a smart dog and always puts his toys away when he's done playing with them."

I turn the page.

"Then I was hoping to have a slide out of Navajo's room so the dogs could slide down into a pool, but not just for fun. It's for practicality."

"Practicality?" My dad's voice chimes in from behind us.

"Yeah. Look here." I turn the page to show my slide-through-dog-wash-station plans.

"The dogs exit here." I point to a drawing of the third-floor door at the top of a long slide. "As they enter the slide, a motion-activated soap dispenser sprays them down. Partway down, soft-bristled brushes and sponges are attached to the sidewalls."

I point to the diagram on the next page. "These will scrub them on the way down. At the bottom, they enter our kiddie pool. They can splash and play in the pool. Then, voilà! They are fed, watered, rested and clean."

I shut my notebook, and Jayda pats me on the back. "Maggie Lou, you are something else!"

"That's what I hear," I reply.

Uncle Bobby walks up hauling two-by-fours on his shoulder.

"So, is anyone else working today? Or should I collect everyone's paycheck on Friday?"

"Calm down, bro," my dad jokes. "This is probably the most work I've seen you do all week."

"And probably the most he'll do all day," Jayda pipes up.

I examine my plans and dwindling pile of scrap lumber, as they all head to the backyard. And suddenly I have a brilliant idea!

I chase after them with my hammer in hand.

"Dad, can I come today?" I follow closely behind him.

"Thought you were busy with Caninetopia?"

"Well, I'm stuck on the design of the automatic water dispenser, and I'm out of scrap lumber."

"Maggie, not today. We're busy."

"But I can help."

"Maggie, we have lots to get done today."

"I could help get it done," I insist, pleading at my dad's back as he loads two-by-fours onto his shoulder.

"Aw, Maggie. I bet you could." Uncle Bobby pinches my cheek annoyingly. I squint at him. "You can carry my lunch pail."

"I can carry more than that, Uncle Boooooooby," I laugh. My dad and Jayda laugh alongside me.

"Chaa," Uncle Bobby snorts. "Sweetie, you couldn't carry a tune."

I drop my hammer "accidentally" on Uncle Bobby's foot, turn to the pile of lumber, quickly hoist three two-by-fours on my shoulder and spin around, barely missing Dad's head and Jayda's Blue Jays cap as I walk straight toward the truck.

I hear them chuckling behind me. My shoulder is killing me, as the load is a tad heavier than I anticipated, but I refuse to stop or to drop this pile anywhere but the back of the truck. I refuse to give Uncle Bobby one more thing to tease me about.

"Métis strong," says Jayda. "You go, brave girl!"

She's right. Keep going, Maggie Lou, I think. *You show them.*

I heave the lumber into the bed of the truck.

"Oh, Maggie." I hear my dad sigh as they all drop lumber in the truck after me.

"Keep repping the double X, Maggie." Jayda ruffles my hair again as Uncle Bobby limps past us. I'm not sure what double X my cousin is referring to, but it sounds cool, like a superhero.

"So, Dad? Can I come?" I continue to trail behind him.

He is now sitting in the driver's seat of the crew truck, trying to ignore me as he goes through papers on his clipboard. Jayda and Bobby jump in while I continue to stand next to my dad so he can't shut the driver's side door.

"I know how to swing a hammer."

"And drop it," jokes Uncle Bobby.

"Not today, Maggie," Dad says he grabs the door handle.

I stare at him, still blocking the door.

"Don't you have school?" Uncle Bobby interjects.

"It's summer holidays, Uncle Booooby," I say. He laughs.

"Just not today," Dad says.

"Just not today?"

"Yes, Maggie. Just not today."

"So. That means tomorrow?"

"I . . . wait . . ." Dad starts. "What?"

"Tomorrow is not today. Soooo. Just not today is tomorrow, and that is when I can go because it's just not today."

Dad is staring at me, his mouth wide open.

"Awesome, thanks, Dad!" I step out of the way so he can shut the door. He is still staring, so I shut it for him.

"Gosh, that girl is smart!" Jayda sits in the back seat. "Think she takes after her cousin."

Dad starts the truck, and it roars like an old lion with a bad cold, coughing and sputtering.

I lean over his open window, smiling.

"Just not today, but tomorrow." I stick my hand into the truck's cab to shake his.

A smile grows across my dad's face.

"Tomorrow." He shakes my hand.

3

TEARING APART OUR BEDROOM, I can barely contain my excitement. I have to find the best possible construction outfit for work tomorrow. I throw most of my sister's clothes on the floor before settling on my own oversized brown Carhartt overalls, a red-and-black plaid button-up shirt and a white undershirt.

All are my cousin Jayda's hand-me-downs.

Rheana enters the room and rolls her big brown judgy eyes at me.

"What is wrong with you?" she asks, kicking clothes out of her way as I lace up my work boots.

"I'm going to work with Dad's construction crew tomorrow."

"And you're wearing those stupid boots to bed?"

"Are you wearing that dumb unicorn onesie to bed?" I snap back.

Rheana pulls the teal unicorn hoodie up over her head. The rainbow horn flops pathetically to one side, making her look even more ridiculous.

"At least it's pajamas. And my feet are not the size of King Kong's!" Rheana crawls into her bunk while staring at my feet. "Oh, my gosh! Whose boots are those? They're filthy!"

"Jayda's. She bought a new pair last month, so I got these." I swish my feet side to side proudly.

"And got whatever sweaty toe fungus she has. EWWWW!" She pulls her pink fleece blanket over her head.

"Want some?" I shake a large dirty boot next to her floppy unicorn horn.

"GROSS!" She pushes my boot away from her face.

"Jayda's sweaty toe fungus . . ." I shake my foot closer as caked dirt falls onto her pillow.

"MOM!" Rheana squeals, batting my leg away, causing me to lose my balance. I tumble onto the heap of clothes on our floor.

Our door opens. Mom is standing there, hands on hips, hair wrapped in a towel, wearing a creepy blue face mask and striped green pajamas.

"What in the world?" she asks, looking around our disaster of a bedroom.

"No doubt, Mom! What in the world?" I ask as Rheana and I stare at the slimy blue putty on her face.

"You never mind. Just clean up this room." She's about to close the door. "And, Maggie, get ready for bed."

"I am!" I exclaim, standing up.

Reopening the door, she stares at me Mom-like, scanning my outfit from top to bottom.

"No, you're not." She starts to close the door again.

"Yes, I am." I start climbing the ladder into my bunk.

The door slowly opens again, and she leans against the doorframe, crossing her arms. Her brown eyes pierce through me like red-hot laser beams.

I stop halfway up the ladder.

"Boots, Maggie?"

"But I go to work in the morning."

"Boots?"

"Yeah. The greatest cousin in the world gave them to me."

"They're dirty."

I look down at them, then jump down with a loud thud and start violently stomping on the floor.

"MAGGIE!" Mom yells.

I look down at the pile of dirt around my feet.

"Not anymore."

"See what I have to live with!?" Rheana says dramatically, rolling herself up like a giant pill bug with a floppy rainbow horn sticking out the top.

Continuing up the ladder, I deliberately tap Rheana on the head with the toe of my boot.

"Pajamas, Maggie," Mom commands and closes the door.

"Yeah, Maggie. Pajamas," Rheana repeats.

Mom reopens the door. "And clean this up before you sleep. One of you will trip in the middle of the night."

"But I work in the morning! I need to get to bed."

Mom shoots me The Look and whispers firmly, "Pajamas. Clean this up."

The door closes, and I understand from her tone of voice not to argue.

In the giant pile of clothes I quickly locate pajamas — an oversized yellow T-shirt with a pug puppy in a red cape flying through the clouds and black lettering that says, *I fart. What's your superpower?*

I love this nightshirt. I pull it over my head, straightening it over my coveralls.

Scanning the room, I see my hockey stick in the corner. I grab it, open our closet door and begin my five-second tidy.

One at a time, I slap-slot several pieces of clothing into the closet. Then I backhand a few under my sister's lower bunk for good measure.

As Rheana peers disgustedly over her blanket at me, I shoot a smelly sock at her head, hitting her right between the eyes.

"SHE SHOOTS! SHE SCORES!" I yell, raising my stick above my head. "AND THE CROWD GOES WILD!"

"The crowd says, Go to bed!" Mom yells through the door.

"Voilà! Room is clean!" I exclaim and drop my

stick in the center of the room.

Rheana pulls her hoodie tightly over her head. "Oh, my gosh, Maggie. You are so annoying. Go to bed."

I take a running start to attempt my one-jump-into-bed maneuver. I land one large boot on the side of Rheana's mattress and spring up into my bunk above hers. Half dangling off and hanging on for dear life, I grasp my blankets and rail to pull myself up. Kicking my legs while inching up like a worm, I finally make it into my bunk.

"Lights?" Rheana calls out from under her hoodie and blanket.

"I got this." I survey my bed and the adjacent shelf. Grabbing a hockey ball, I aim it at the light switch.

SWOOSH. I let it go.

BANG. It hits the wall just to the left of the switch.

I toss another one, which lands just to the right of the light switch.

BANG.

"Hang on." I grab a hockey puck off the shelf.

Lining it up with the light switch, I toss it in the air with a quick flick of my wrist just as our door opens again.

Dez peeks his head in. "What's with all the —"

SWOOSH.

Dez's lightning-fast reflexes allow him to duck just as the puck flies out the door.

". . . noise?" he continues as the puck hits the wall behind him with a BOOM.

"BED!" We hear the shout from our parents' room.

Dez laughs as he's about to shut our door.

"Light, please." Rheana calls from her bunk.

"Sure thing. Goodnight, girls." And he switches off the light.

"Thanks, Dez," I call out, lying back in my bunk.

He turns the light back on and quickly slams the door, calling from the other side, "No prob."

We hear him whistling down the hall toward his bedroom.

Sighing loudly, Rheana unrolls herself and stumbles to the switch to turn off the light.

"Thanks," I say politely. I pull my blanket up over

my boots and tuck it under my chin, wondering what great and mighty things I will build tomorrow.

Suddenly, my eyes snap open and I whip myself into a sitting position, gasping and panicking.

MY TOOLS!

4

"OOF!"

Early the next morning my work boots fight to get loose from the blankets. I roll off my top bunk.

THUMP. My body hits the floor.

BANG! CLANG! My tool belt and a few random tools land hard around me.

"Maaaaggggiiieee," moans Rheana.

"Shhh!" I whisper as I struggle to untangle my boots from the blanket, kicking at the floor.

The door snaps open.

"Mmmwha?" Mom mumbles. She's wearing nursing scrubs and brushing her teeth. Her eyes dart around the floor, surveying the mess around me.

". . . haats appenen?" she gurgles through a mouthful of toothpaste.

"Nothing, Mom." I start to gather my tools and stand up, kicking my blanket into the corner of the room.

I pull the yellow pajama shirt over my head and toss it onto Rheana's face.

"Just a few things I need for work." I flip my bedhead side to side as I try to fasten the toolbelt around my waist.

"She kept me up all night, Mom," Rheana groans from under my nightshirt, tossing it back at me. "Up and down. Down and up. She's so loud."

"I needed my TOOOOOOLLLS!" I straighten my toolbelt. "Some of us are going to build this world into a better place today . . . while others will be sleeping their life away."

I shake my head, peering through my hair.

Mom wipes the side of her mouth with the back of her hand.

"Yur a weck aggie ou . . . cean up," she mumbles.

"Yeah, I know, Mom. Love you, too."

Shaking her head side to side, she sprays green foam as she spins and walks away.

I gather my tools from the floor. My hammer,

my Phillips screwdriver with the x-shaped head, a flathead screwdriver. I place each into one of the leather loops on my toolbelt. I find my measuring tape, work gloves and carpenter's pencil, which is bigger than a regular pencil and flat so it can be tucked behind your ear. I stash both in the front pouch.

I tie my hair back in a messy bun. Ready for whatever work throws my way, I stomp my boots and make my way to the kitchen.

The smell of coffee wafts down the hall. As I enter the kitchen, Uncle Bobby and Jayda are laughing with my dad while getting ready for the workday.

"Well, look what the bear dragged in!" Uncle Bobby exclaims. "If it isn't Tomorrow and Not Today."

"Mornin' Mags," Jayda sputters through a mouthful of toast and peanut butter. Crumbs drop from her lips onto her AC/DC T-shirt.

"Morning!" I grab a glass of OJ.

"Better have something more than that," Dad chuckles and hands me a bowl of oatmeal. "Ya need something to stick to those ribs."

I sit on a stool at the island counter and shovel in the oatmeal as I listen to the chatter flying around the room. Mom comes in and kicks Uncle Bobby's boots off the edge of the table.

"What the heck, Bobby?" she says crossly as she storms past him to the door.

"Sorry," he answers.

"Kiss for good luck?" Dad walks over to Mom as she slips her shoes on.

"I'm going to be late."

Leaning in, he winks at her. "Okay, a kiss for being late."

She pecks him on the cheek and pokes him in the chest with her finger.

"Take care of Maggie Lou today, Elvis. I don't want to see her down at the ER!" She grabs her lunch kit and turns to leave.

Dad whips Mom around in his arms, dips her backward and plants a big kiss on her lips, knocking her lunch kit from her hand.

Everyone but me cheers.

"Still got it, Elvis!" Uncle Bobby yells.

Mom straightens herself and shoos him away in

Michif. "*Awas!*" She grabs her lunch, opens the door and leaves, winking at Dad.

Ewww. I look back down at my oatmeal bowl.

"Okay, boys and girls." Dad smiles at me. "Gather yourselves. It's time to put to use what the good Creator gave you!" He grabs his lunch box and coffee thermos from the counter.

"And what's that?" Uncle Bobby asks, laughing.

"Strong backs and weak minds!" chuckles my older brother Vince from behind us.

"Holay! Finally gets here." Jayda shakes her head.

"No doubt. Welcome to work, Sleeping Beauty." Uncle Bobby grabs the last chocolate chip muffin from the plate and takes a giant bite.

"Did you hear about the three electricians and the carpenter?" Vince asks as we all stare blankly at him. "The three electricians walked into a bar, but the carpenter ducked." Vince's laughter is the only sound that fills the kitchen. As he walks past Uncle Bobby, he snatches the muffin out of his hand and heads out the back door.

"HEY!" Bobby yells.

"It's the breakfast of champions," Vince yells

back. "So you won't be needing it!"

The room breaks into laughter as everyone gathers their belongings and heads out to the trucks. With every tool we load into the back, I imagine myself using it to build my great and wonderful Caninetopia! I can slice two-by-fours into pieces with the circular saw. As I walk with the electric sander in my hands, I imagine sanding down the flooring and painting a cool design in the center. Uncle Bobby hauls a miter saw to cut angles and corners, so I'll definitely need to use that. Jayda carries an air compressor and air nailer. It makes loud noises and shoots nails right through the wood so much faster than my hammer.

There are so many tools to learn how to use and so many things to build. I can't wait!

Not today but tomorrow is starting off great!

5

ARRIVING AT THE WORK SITE feels magical. It's full of construction crews, machinery, noise and a lot of dust.

It's a small cul-de-sac in a new suburb on the edge of the city. It's a busy place, and I can't stop staring. Cement trucks are busy making driveways, a Bobcat is digging in a nearby yard and a large dump truck beeps as it backs up.

Our crews are working on four houses, each a different style and at a different stage of construction.

Another truck arrives behind us with more cousins who work with us. The workers get out of their vehicles. They already know their assignments, so they unload the trailers and truck beds, then head into different houses.

I wonder what great things I'll learn to build today. Maybe I'll help them with a winding stairwell. Then I could make one inside Caninetopia. Or maybe they'll show me how to make a back patio with a pergola. I could make a small deck off the back of my dog mansion, hang some lights, and the dogs could have an ultra-cool place to lie out.

The possibilities are endless!

"Okay, my girl, follow me."

I follow my dad as he carries tools into the house on the corner lot. It's a raised bungalow and is nearing what is called lock-up stage, which means the skeleton of the house is complete, and the interior and finishing carpentry will come next.

The earthy smell of fresh sawdust fills my nostrils as we enter.

Building is in my blood. I can feel it.

Dad places the supplies he's carrying in the middle of the floor. Some of the guys are cutting downstairs, and the sound of their saws is music to my ears.

As I set down my lunch bag and water bottle, I notice it's pretty dirty and messy here. Along with all the sawdust and dirt are empty boxes, plastic wrap, old food containers and crumpled-up pop cans.

"Welcome to tomorrow not today, Maggie Lou. Your introductory course to house construction," Dad jokes as he hands me a large black garbage bag and a broom.

Dad leans the broom against me and puts the garbage bag on my shoulder as I stand there with my mouth gaping.

"You can start here today. Your brother's crews are as bad as his jokes. Jayda's crew on the other hand . . . let's just say she runs a tight ship!"

He kicks an empty pop bottle out of his way. "We need this cleaned up before we start insulating and finishing."

Uncle Bobby walks up from the basement. "Okay, Elvis, my work here is done. On to the next one."

"Thanks, Lastcall."

Uncle Bobby is the electrician on my dad's crew. Everyone jokes that he's not needed until all the real work is done. That's how he earned his nickname, because he's the last one called to the job site.

"Ha-ha. Well, without me, you have no power."

I look ridiculous.

These guys think they are so funny! I untie the blue recycling bag, pick up my broom and start to clean the room, hoping no one else saw me sleeping on the floor.

I sort cans and bottles into the blue bag, cardboard into the green bag, then garbage into the black bag. I sort random pieces of lumber and plywood, place them at the edge of the room and sweep up the mounds of sawdust.

Dad walks in a short time later and scans the room.

"Lunchtime, Molasses."

"What?"

"You, my girl." He smiles at me. "Molasses. Just a little slow this morning, but that's okay. You'll pick up the pace after some lunch."

"Yeah, sure." I grab my lunch bag and water bottle and follow him out the door.

The crews gather outside for lunch, sitting on the endgates of the trucks or on the trailer beds. It's like a construction-site picnic.

I sit cross-legged in the bed of the truck eating

my peanut butter and pickle sandwich, the ultimate combination of sweet and salty. This is my next favorite sandwich after a gooey melted cheese.

"What did the grape say when he got stepped on?" Vince asks as he tosses a green grape into the air and catches it in his mouth. "He let out a small wine!" Everyone continues to dig into their lunches as he laughs all by himself.

I listen to the workers talk and laugh about their weekends suffer through a few more of my brother's corny jokes, and it's fun until Jayda instructs me to cover my ears during some parts of the conversations. Guys are so weird, I think.

I'm so happy Jayda is here. She's always looking out for me, and she plays excellent pranks on the guys.

I finish my apple and the fizzy orange drink my mom packed for me, saving my cookies for our afternoon coffee break.

"Okay, boys and girls." My dad winks at me. "Time is money, and we're not making any sittin' around. Let's get atter."

I head back to the house. I grab the broom and

move to the other rooms and the hall. Partway through the afternoon, I search for my dad to find more bags. I toss the full black one into the red bin outside and the full blue one into the back of the truck.

As I return to the house, my cousins Dustin and Kenyon, who have been working downstairs, start carrying their tools out.

As they pass me on the stairs, one says, "We're all done. You can go nap downstairs." And they shut the door, laughing.

Bunch of comedians these guys are, I think as I walk down to the basement.

I stop at the bottom of the stairs, and my mouth drops open. It is a disaster worse than my bedroom. There's moldy food in containers. In the middle of the room, there's a giant pyramid taller than me made of empty cans and bottles. Torn-up plastic wrapping and cardboard cover the floor like fall leaves but not as pretty.

Working through our crew's second coffee break, I fill two more garbage bags, three blue bags and two green bags. I finish cleaning the basement and gather two large piles of scrap lumber. Walking out of the house, excited to be done this glamorous job, I hope I never see another broom.

"All done, my girl?"

"Yep." I hurl the last bag into the red bin.

"And the scrap lumber?"

"It's inside."

"Well, it has to get tossed into the chipper. See that yellow machine Lastcall's feeding?"

He points at Uncle Bobby, who's throwing scrap lumber into a large, noisy machine in the center of the yard.

"Yeah." I'm about as excited as Musqua when I try to throw a ball for him. He just stares at me, then lies down and waits for Navajo to retrieve it instead.

"It's all gotta get thrown in there. Lastcall will help you."

I drag myself into the house and examine the large pile of scrap lumber upstairs. I stare down the long stairwell.

I kick a random piece of wood, and it tumbles down.

Suddenly I remember the slide in Caninetopia,

and I have a brilliant idea!

Grabbing some broken sheets of plywood, I start to construct a slide down the stairwell. I find some scrap two-by-fours and attach them to the sides of the plywood to act as bumpers, just like a bowling alley where my family played once. It had bumpers to stop the balls from rolling into the gutter.

I toss a couple of pieces down.

DONK! BANG! TING!

The pieces pile up at the bottom of the stairs.

I stand with my hands on my hips, wondering what I can do to get rid of this new pile.

I think about building a conveyor belt to the wood chipper, but that's too far.

Ah-ha!

Scanning the yard, I notice an empty wheelbarrow. I run down my makeshift lumber slide, careful not to trip and land face-first. Then I dash across the yard to grab the wheelbarrow.

I quickly roll it back to the house, prop open the front door and set the wheelbarrow at the end of the slide. I find a few four-by-four scrap posts around the same length. I remove a few sheets of broken plywood from the bottom of the lumber slide and use the pieces of four-by-four to create a platform that matches the height of the wheelbarrow. I hammer the plywood back into place over top of the four-by-four frame and roll the wheelbarrow beneath the edge of the slide.

"VOILÀ!"

I run up the slide and start tossing scrap lumber down it.

BANG! TING! DONK!

Boards slide and tumble down one by one, hitting the two-by-four bumpers on their way. With loud crashing noises, they hit the metal wheelbarrow at the bottom. Slowly the large pile of scrap lumber upstairs shrinks.

Once the wheelbarrow is half full, I slide down, grab the handles and push the heavy load over to the wood chipper.

I yell at Uncle Bobby over the loud yellow machine, "ORDER UP!"

Bobby turns around and smiles.

"Work smarter, not harder, eh?"

I nod, happy with my invention. He pulls a pair

of clear safety glasses and colorful foam earplugs from his pocket.

"Safety first, my girl."

I scrunch up my nose because the glasses look ugly and earplugs are uncomfortable. But my dad is strict about safety, and we'd both be in heaps of trouble if either of us were caught without them.

Bobby explains how to use the chipper and which scraps to keep. Any pieces longer than three feet should be saved. I rescue some sheets of plywood and trim boards I think will work well in Caninetopia.

Uncle Bobby and I take turns tossing scraps into the chipper. When the wheelbarrow is empty, I run back to the house to refill it.

But by the third load, I just want to go home. Uncle Bobby tells me to dismantle my lumber slide and throw it in as well.

I look at my watch. It's 4:30.

I grab my lunch bag and toss it into the back of the truck.

"HEY! MAGGIE!" I hear my dad from across the street.

"What?"

"Don't forget the scraps from around the outside of the house." He smiles and gives me two big thumbs up. "Thirty minutes left, my girl!"

My feet drag as I turn around and grab the wheelbarrow. My hands ache as I squeeze the handles, feeling small blisters forming on my index fingers. I scour the yard for more scrap lumber. I fill two more wheelbarrows and get more slivers in my hands and wish I'd worn the gloves Dad gave me. I stand at the corner of the house, trying to pull out the tiny wood slivers.

Finally, I hear the blast of the truck horn.

HOOONNNK HOOONNNK.

"Pack it up! Pack it in!" Dad roars.

"Let me begin!" a few of them answer. Then, like a well-practiced Rabbit Dance, everyone begins to pack up tools, shut doors, load trailers, and we are in the trucks at 5:15 on the dot.

Dad looks at me in the rearview mirror, smiling as I lean my head against the back window. I'm tired and hungry.

"How was just not today but tomorrow, my girl?"

"Meh. Not as exciting as I thought it would be."

"Such is life," Uncle Bobby states between bites of a chocolate doughnut.

"But guess what?" Dad continues.

I peer up at him through my drooping eyes, too exhausted to lift my head.

"Tomorrow is not today either. Soooo. Same bat time, same bat channel." Dad starts the truck, and it growls like an old lion.

Laughing, he hits the gas, and we head for home.

6

BANG BANG BANG.

Dad whips open the bedroom door, shining the hall light into my face.

"Rise and shine, sleepyhead. Your crew awaits your arrival."

I squint at my clock. How did 7:30 come so quickly? I'm positive I just laid down my head.

It's week three of my construction adventure, and it has been the worst time of my life. My body is sore. My feet ache. My hands are covered in slivers and scars.

I dangle my legs off the bunk and let them just hang there for a moment, trying to think of an excuse for why I cannot go to work today.

But I can't think of one that will work with my

dad. He believes there is no excuse not to work, unless you are in the hospital or dead. And tired as I am, I don't think I'm near either.

I lie face down, thinking about all the work I've done. I've cleaned three of the four houses, picked and sorted good lumber from bad, put scraps through the chipper and pulled more nails than I ever imagined possible. I even replaced toilet paper and hand sanitizer in the smelly blue outhouses. One afternoon I watched the entire crew drive away "to go get screws they forgot," as I was left behind to "hand-bomb," which means empty a trailer full of two-by-fours by hand all by myself.

Then they all returned with doughnuts instead of screws, and Vince told me, "Whatever doesn't kill you makes you not die," laughing as he walked away.

Jayda was behind him. She pulled a doughnut wrapped in a napkin out of her pocket. She handed it to me and whispered, "Stay strong and brave, double X."

Doughnut or no doughnut, I want to quit every single day. But I refuse to be known as a quitter, so here I am hanging onto the edge of my bed, thanking the Creator that it's finally Friday.

I slip off my top bunk, landing with a loud THUD.

"Hey, Construction Cathy."

I crane my head to see Dez leaning against the doorway, eating a slice of leftover pizza for breakfast.

"So. Heard you're the crew's best daytime sleeper." As he laughs, I see mushed-up pizza moving around inside his mouth.

Boys are so gross, especially younger brothers.

"Yeah, well, at least I'm the best at something other than being annoying." I toss a dirty sock at him. "And the smelliest boy in town."

Gathering my tools and fastening my belt, I ignore Dez's trail of pizza crumbs at the entrance to my bedroom.

"You can leave those tools behind. From what I hear, all you need are garbage bags and your sweet mode of transportation," he snorts. "Your broom!" Bursting out in laughter, he turns to walk away.

Lining up with the back of his giant head, I grab

a wet towel from our floor and whip it at him.

SMACK.

"Score!" I yell loudly, then finish tying my boots.

WHACK.

A pillow knocks me in the back of my head.

"Quiet! Maggie!" Rheana screeches from her bottom bunk and rolls herself up in her blanket.

"Go back to sleep, you pest." I kick her pillow out into the hallway as I make my way to the kitchen.

"SHUT THE DOOR!" she yells.

"YOU SHUT IT!"

"Shut what?" Dad raises his eyebrows as I enter the kitchen.

"Nothing, Dad." I grab a muffin from the counter.

"Good. Everyone is loading up the trucks. Let's get this show on the road, Construction Cathy!" He turns his head and yells, "DEZ! Let's go!"

"Dez?" I ask between bites as I follow him out the door.

"Yes, your brother's gonna help out today. We have a lot to do. It's Friday."

Jumping into the truck, I sink into my seat, dreading the next eight hours.

Not only do I have to clean, but I also have to put up with my brother!

I close my eyes, waiting for the longest day of my life to begin.

* * *

Arriving at the busy construction site today is nowhere near as magical as my first day. My dreams have been crushed, chipped, sawed in half and bagged. We go through the same motions every day. Unload, unpack and begin our duties. Dad instructs me to take Dez to the last house and start cleaning.

Sighing heavily, I grab a few bags of each color from the back of the truck.

As I turn to head over to the house, Dez runs past me, riding the broom.

"Hey, sis! Gonna borrow your ride!"

I hope he trips, I think.

"VROOOOM!" He makes driving noises as he runs toward the house.

Once inside, I hand Dez the bags one at a time,

giving him clear instructions about what needs to be done.

We've begun to sort through the mess when Dad appears.

"So, Maggie? You think he's ready?"

"Sure, Dad, whatever."

"To be on his own? You think we can trust him?"

My eyes light up.

"Yes!" I answer.

"Good. Grab your belt. Let's go build something." And he winks at me.

I toss my brother the broom and run up behind Dad without missing a beat.

"HEY! That's not fair!" I hear Dez yell.

"Gotta start somewhere, my boy," Dad answers.

"I'm no maid!" Dez continues.

"And you're no master builder, either. Hafta learn the ropes, son!"

Dad and I walk into the first house where I worked during my first week, and I no longer recognize it. The bare two-by-fours between the rooms are now covered with drywall, and doorways have been roughed in. Walls divide the space into rooms, and there's now a ceiling instead of just rafters.

It looks much more like a house than the mess I remember.

"Well, Maggie, what do you think?"

"It's amazing!" I shout, wandering from room to room.

"Thank you," Jayda says as she leaves the back bedroom, toolbox in hand.

"You did all this?" I ask.

"Well, of course! You don't think these guys could make all this magic happen alone, do you?" she laughs, walking to the front door. "Off to the next one. Have fun, Maggie! And remember, always be willing to step out of the box!"

She winks at me as she leaves.

"She's right," Dad says. "The fun has only begun. Now all the good stuff happens. The finishing."

He grabs a box that holds many different samples and tosses it to me.

"What's your eye telling you for this house?" he asks.

"Really? I get to choose?"

I grab the box of samples, and it's like Christmas

for my small builder's heart. It's like building with Legos or my crazy inventions in our yard. Only this is so much better because it's a real house!

I pull out samples, laying them out on the floor one by one. Dad shows me how to hold paint swatches next to the window to see them in natural light. He and I go through all the samples for flooring, cupboards, countertops, hardware, railings, paint, trim boards and pictures of light fixtures and doors. He explains how to overlap the samples on each other to see how they look together.

This is so different than building a bike ramp out of leftover construction scraps or trying to design Caninetopia on paper.

This feels like my dream job!

Dad and I spend a few hours picking and choosing, discussing the differences between good and poor choices and why. He teaches me about flooring, sub-flooring, paint colors and types, countertops and doors.

Who knew there were so many kinds of doors? There are panel doors, shaker doors, sliding doors, barn doors, folding doors, pocket doors.

All this new information makes me dizzy, but I drink it all in.

At noon we check on Dez. He is lying on his back in the middle of the floor with his hat over his face, snoring.

Dad is about to wake him when I motion for him to *shhh*.

I quietly grab the blue recycling bag from the middle of the room. We carefully slide it through Dez's front belt loops, tie it in a giant bow and sneak away.

Winking at me, Dad announces to the crew that we are leaving to buy some nails he forgot. He grabs all the samples we selected, and we jump into his truck.

Stopping for coffee and doughnuts is our first order of business.

I feel like I have been promoted!

With my armful of samples, I strut next to my dad toward the order desk at the back of the building supply store. The order desk clerk is wearing a name tag that says *Connie*.

"So, this is Maggie Lou?"

I nod proudly.

"I've heard all about you. Your dad says you're a great worker like your cousin Jayda. And from the looks of it, you may be the best decorator he's had." She smiles as she sorts through the samples. She writes all our selections on a form and compliments my choices.

Dad places his arm around my shoulders.

"Settle down, Connie. Let's not get carried away. She's not taking over the business."

"Yet," she says with a grin. "Pickup is in the back. Most of your selections are here, except for that gorgeous kitchen sink." She nods. "Great choice, Maggie Lou."

Dad signs some papers, thanks Connie, and we head off to pick up our supplies.

Arriving back at the construction site is even more magical than the first day I arrived.

As I help carry each box of materials into the house, I think it's incredible that I'm helping to create someone's home. I now understand why my family loves this business.

* * *

Saturday morning, Dad decides we will work overtime. Dez is back on cleaning duty, and I'm partnered with Dad to install some of the supplies we bought yesterday. Dad says we need to paint before we start on the flooring.

By noon, the paint on the bedroom walls is dry. Then after lunch break, we begin to lay flooring. Dad teaches me the importance of measuring twice and only cutting once as we place it board by board. We carefully interlock each piece, using a rubber mallet to fit them together. I listen carefully to Dad. He says we cannot be impatient during this part of the job.

Cutting my first board is a fantastic feeling. I learn how to read the different lines on the measuring tape — what 1/8 is and how to find 5/8 of an inch. He teaches me how to properly use a miter saw and the other cool tools on the job.

It's like assembling a giant jigsaw puzzle, only better.

And Dad lets me keep some scrap lumber and leftover flooring for Caninetopia! I am even more excited about that project, as I now understand how to improve my plans based on what I've learned here this week. I think I'm going to add a front porch and sundeck on the roof!

Go big or go home is my new motto.

We work together as a team, and the hours fly by. I feel like a light bulb is glowing above my head all day! I am shocked when Dad announces it is five o'clock and time to call it a day.

That night I lie in my top bunk, reviewing everything I've done in the past few weeks. All the lessons I've learned are precious, slivers and all. Even working with Dez wasn't as awful as I thought it would be. He's not always completely annoying. Like the rest of my family, he's actually funny, and I now even enjoy hanging out with him once in a while.

I just don't tell him that.

Dad informs me that it's Rheana's turn to join us next week, and I get to show her the ropes! I'm so excited to boss her around. I mean, instruct her on what needs to get done on the work site.

I guess Dad is right. Building things must run in our blood!

THREE

PRAIRIEWALKER, SISTER OF BUSHWALKER

1

"GOOD SHOOTING, MY GIRL!" Dad ruffles my hair.

Uncle Bobby leans out the driver's side window of his truck.

"Not too shabby, little Maggie," he yells.

We are all target shooting at his farm, where Uncle Bobby has set up a shooting range at the back of his eighty acres.

The range is a long, narrow strip of land lined by pine trees, and there are no neighbors for miles. It used to be a smelly slough that dried up long ago. Uncle says it's not suitable for planting, so it's a great location for a shooting range. He set up a picnic table where we can load our weapons and shoot from one end of the range.

At the other end he built a couple of wooden

frames to hold our paper targets.

We've been doing target shooting as a family for as long as I can remember. It usually turns into some type of competition. I was five years old when I shot my first bow.

Every Thanksgiving, it's a family tradition to do a turkey shoot using bows. We shoot at a life-sized rubber turkey, and the winner receives a giant chocolate turkey and our family's prized turkey trophy, which used to be one of Moshôm's old curling trophies. Mom turned the sliding curler on the top into a turkey by gluing on pieces of old Christmas ornaments and feathers in the shape of a bird.

Mom is very creative. That's probably where I get it from.

I haven't won the turkey shoot yet, but my little brother Dez has, and he holds that particular Thanksgiving Day over my head every year. He is such a brat.

I flip the safety on my .22 rifle and place the gun in its case.

As I walk down the range to the targets, my cousin Jayda suddenly whips up beside me.

"I bet you got it this time, squirt!" She knocks my baseball cap off my head and runs ahead of me. I ignore my cap and race her to the targets.

Jayda beats me by a mile. She rips the paper off the frame, examines it and then holds it above her head.

"Annie Oakley over here!"

I run to her and jump up as she holds the sheet of paper out of my reach.

"Let me see, Jayda!"

She takes off back to the family standing at the end of the range. I'm right on her tail, trying to catch up with her wild dreads flying behind her in the wind

She beats me again.

Jayda hands the paper to Moshôm, who is sitting at the picnic table. He examines it through his reading glasses. He nods his head slowly and hands it to Kohkom.

I stand beside them, waiting.

"*Kwayes kitôtîn*, my girl!" Kohkom pulls me in for a big squishy hug. "You did good. Looks like we have another hunter in the family."

She hands me the target paper. Mom and Dad stand next to me to examine it as well.

"That's my girl, Maggie." Mom pats me on the back.

"Looks like you're ready for the big guns." Dad smiles.

Dez runs up and snatches the target from my hands.

"First we need to measure!" He runs to Uncle Bobby's truck and grabs a measuring tape from the toolbox in the back. Laying the paper on the hood, Dez carefully measures the five holes I've made.

"Sorry, my boy," Uncle Bobby says from the driver's seat. "You could remeasure it all day. She did it. Better luck next time, Dez."

Dez has been trying to beat me at target practice all summer.

"Oh, whatever." Dez tosses my paper to the ground. "Doesn't mean anything."

After we turn thirteen and prove that we can shoot five bullets into a small area on a target — the adults call it a two-inch grouping — we can join them as hunters.

It has taken SO MUCH practice, but now I can do it. Dez is just jealous that I get to go hunting this year, while he has to wait three more years. HA-HA! Sucks to be the baby!

Scooping the target from the ground, I smile. "It means I get to shoot the big guns now, little man."

Rheana sits up in the back seat of Uncle Bobby's truck, where she's been reading one of her silly teen magazines.

"Oh, my gosh! Are we almost done? I'm hungry."

"Don't worry, sis! Soon I will fill our freezer full of deer!" I throw my target at her. "Read it and weep!"

"Big deal." She rolls her eyes. "You can shoot. Congrats." Rheana tosses the target back out the window, lies down again and yells, "If anyone cares, there's a starving girl in the back seat of this smelly truck. Just lying here, wasting away."

"You're so overdramatic." I pick up my target from the ground again.

"*Kitakahkowîpin'kân*, Maggie Lou," Vince shouts from the picnic table. That means you did good in Michif.

"Thanks, brother."

"But do you know what kind of gun a military chef uses?" Vince starts laughing at his joke before the punchline. "Assault rifle! Get it? A salt rifle!" We stare at him in silence as he slaps his knee.

I come from a long line of hunters. When I was young, I started using slingshots, then moved on to bows and pellet guns. My grandparents bought me a .22 rifle for my tenth birthday.

Almost everyone in my family hunts — or wants to — except Rheana.

I don't understand her at all. This summer was especially exciting because I was finally able to take the Hunter Safety Course and I passed!

"Okay, Maggie. Come learn to load my Winchester," Mom calls.

"Wait! Can't have you be the only one representing the double X today!" Jayda shouts, loading her 12-gauge shotgun. "Pigeons up, Bobby!"

She marches toward the shooting line. Uncle Bobby prepares a clay target in the thrower. It works like a pitching machine, but instead of hurling baseballs, it tosses the clay targets high into the air.

"Ready?" he calls out, tugging back on the hinge.

Jayda turns her baseball cap backward, steadies herself and pulls her shotgun tight to her shoulder.

Leaning her head to the side, she stares up at the sky in front of her and yells, "PULL!"

SNAP WHIP WHIZZ!

A clay target flies high into the air in front of her. She waits until it hits the highest point, then . . .

BOOM!

She pulls the trigger.

SMASH!

Jayda pulls quickly on the rifle's pump action, loading another shell into the chamber as the clay pigeon explodes into three pieces high in the sky.

BANG!

She shoots again, hitting one of the pieces as it falls and reloads another shell.

POW!

Before the last piece can land, she blasts it to smithereens.

Turning around, she winks at me. "It just runs in our blood, little Maggie."

"Show-off," Vince comments as he gets up from the table.

"Oh? You gonna show me up, Vince?" Jayda teases, offering him her shotgun.

"I would, but I hurt my arm this week." Vince rolls his shoulder.

"Doing what?" she laughs, putting her shotgun away.

"Leaning my elbows on the table all week waiting to get paid." He looks at Dad.

"Congrats," Dad jokes. "You now have the highest cheekbones in the family. Good job, son."

This summer has been the best!

I've spent it working with Dad's construction company, and Jayda stole me from Dad's crew to work with her. She said Uncle Bobby would lead me astray, trying to talk me into learning electrical work. Besides, she says we girls need to stick together. I had such a great summer working for her, learning about building and being a boss lady.

I also learned how to use a 20-gauge shotgun. On my thirteenth birthday, Uncle Bobby and Vince took me out to learn. It's the smallest shotgun we own, and they said I should practice so I can use it for hunting ducks and geese.

I'll never forget that day! The shotgun's powerful recoil bruised my shoulder, and its loud blasts made my ears ring all day. Vince told me to ice my shoulder because I was still complaining about the pain when we returned home. Mom gave them heck for not instructing me correctly. I was used to my .22 rifle, which barely moves when fired, but shotguns are different! My uncle and brother didn't warn me that I should hold the butt-end of the gun firmly against my shoulder, so that my body could absorb its impact.

Either way, I loved it. Uncle Bobby hurled the clay into the air while Vince stood next to me, instructing me to aim a little ahead of the target's path.

Then suddenly his booming voice shouted, "SHOOT 'EM!"

He would startle me, but I'd shoot, and seeing the clay pigeon bust into a hundred pieces mid-air was amazing.

My goal is to shoot like Jayda. She's so awesome. She always watches out for me when I get my crazy ideas. Like the time I made a ramp for my skateboard that went from our front porch all the way down to the end of our sidewalk. She caught me before I left the porch and asked me what I would do if I flew off the end of the sidewalk into oncoming traffic.

In all my excitement, I forgot about the dangers.

But it happens to the best of us.

Like on one cold, windy fall day out at Uncle Bobby's acreage, he and my dad wanted to shoot targets with Dez but were trying to avoid going outside.

I stood at the kitchen counter, slowly eating a bag of chips as they set themselves up in Uncle Bobby's kitchen. Uncle set up targets in the yard while Dad moved the kitchen table and chair in front of the window.

I watched as Uncle Bobby pulled off the screen and sat Dez at the table with his Red Ryder BB gun so he could shoot the targets from the window.

As Dez took aim, Mom yelled from the other room, "I don't think this idea of yours is …"

BAM!

"… a good one," she finished.

Dez's eyes grew as big as Kohkom's bannocks as

he clutched the pellet gun.

His shot had put a hole in the wooden window frame!

Dad and Uncle Bobby thought it was hilarious, but Mom was angry. She took away the BB gun, scolded the three shooters like they were all children, then made them stand outside in the cold to think about what they had done.

Mom's method of teaching us to think before we act is pretty effective.

"Half-time show is over, Jayda. Time for everyone else to get a turn," Dad calls out now.

"Here ya go, Maggie."

Mom hands me her pride and joy, her Winchester .308. Dad bought it for her birthday when she started hunting eight years ago, and now they hunt together every fall. We kids call it "orphan season," because once hunting season opens, we don't see anyone but Kohkom and Moshôm until everyone has filled their tags. Anyone who comes up empty-handed takes what our family calls the walk of shame and has to eat tag soup.

The most frequent victim is Vince, whom Mom

has nicknamed Bushwalker. She says thank goodness Vince knows where to hunt bologna sandwiches, or he'd be a Starvin' Marvin.

I stand beside the picnic table, carefully holding Mom's Winchester as she explains how to load it. I need to use a little force to push the shells down on top of each another. Her rifle holds four in the clip and one in the chamber.

"*Âstam*, my girl." Kohkom pats the seat beside her at the picnic table. "You start here to stay steady."

She and Moshôm stand so I can sit. Mom stands to my right, Jayda comes to my left and Kohkom stands behind me.

I like being surrounded by the women in our family. They are all so strong. According to my dad, the men in the family have to be "tough sons of guns, 'cause look what we are up against."

"Lean in and steady yourself. Hold the butt tight to your shoulder." I feel my mom's hand on my back. "Line up the sights to the center. Breathe." She removes her hand.

"Remember, shoot between the sounds of your heartbeat," Jayda whispers behind me.

I slow my breathing as I feel the sweat drip down the back of my neck. I line up the crosshairs to the center black dot on the new target posted at the end of the range.

TA-TUMP TA-TUMP TA-TUMP.

My heart beats loudly in my ears. I hold gentle pressure on the trigger.

I am waiting for the right moment.

TA-TUMP.

And *BOOM.*

Right between heartbeats, I squeeze the trigger.

I immediately draw back on the bolt, load another round in the chamber and stare through the scope at the target.

"Like a pro!" Jayda exclaims and smacks me on the back.

"Like boring!" Rheana calls from the back seat of the truck. "Are we done yet?"

I ignore my sister as I try to locate my shot on the paper.

"Five inches to the left!" Dad calls out. He's leaning against the truck, looking down the range through his binoculars.

"HOLAY! You gonna be having tag soup this season, sis!" Dez yells from the hood of the truck where he's lying against the windshield.

"Don't worry about them," Mom says. "You know how to correct your shot. Just like with your .22."

I reposition myself.

"Breathe," Kohkom whispers.

I take a deep breath, close my left eye and focus right down the center of the scope. Pulling the rifle in close, I begin the process all over again.

TA-TUM TA-TUM.

BOOM!

Mom's Winchester has a slight kick but is not as forceful as the shotgun. I pull on the bolt, reload again and stare down at the target through the scope.

"Two inches to the right!" Dad calls out.

"BAW HAW HAW!" Dez's laughter rings out from the hood of Uncle's truck. "We're all gonna be Starvin' Marvins this fall!"

SWISH SWISH SWOOSH SPLASH.

Uncle Bobby turns on the windshield wipers, spraying Dez.

"Hey!" Dez calls out, jumping off the hood.

Jayda taps me on the back. "Come on, Maggie."

I shake my shoulders to relax them and reposition myself on the picnic table bench. I take a deep breath and do what my kohkom has taught me to do when I'm nervous. She says to close my eyes and create what I want to happen within my mind, so it becomes real to my body. She says if my mind believes it can happen, my body will believe it, too.

I close my eyes, imagining the shot. In my mind I see the bullet fly from the end of the barrel, breaking the paper at the end and BULLSEYE!

I open my eyes and focus.

TA-TUM TA-TUM TA-TUM.

I squeeze the trigger.

BOOM!

"Third time's the charm!" Dad shouts.

Peering through the scope, I can see the target, and where the bullet has struck.

I hit just above the top right corner of the bullseye.

Mom wraps her arm around me. "I see deer steak in your future, my girl."

Kohkom pats my shoulder.

"Apple doesn't fall far from the tree. That's enough for today. Let's go eat!"

Disappointed, I drop my head. I was looking forward to making the rest of my shots.

"Next week." She nods her head at me like she knows what I'm thinking.

"Oh, my goodness! *Marrsî*, Kohkom! Finally, someone hears my pain!" Rheana sits up in the back seat.

"The only pain you are, Rheana, is in the b —"

I feel Kohkom's gentle hand on my shoulder.

". . . beautiful. You're a pain in the beautiful." My voice trails off. ". . . beautiful rump of a donkey," I mumble to myself as I empty the remaining shells, and Mom packs the rifle safely in its case.

We all jump into the bed of the truck like a herd of animals. When all of us are seated, Jayda smacks the rear window.

"Locked and loaded!" she hollers, and Uncle Bobby drives slowly through the bumpy field to his house.

I'm sitting next to Jayda, tightly clutching my

target sheets. I hold them up to the sky and peer through the holes in the paper, smiling.

THWRAP THUMP.

Uncle hits a huge bump.

"Keep your legs and arms in the ride at all times!" he yells.

SWOOSH.

As I come down from the bump, the wind suddenly picks up, and my paper flies from my hands into the air.

"MY TARGETS!" I attempt to reach it as it sails out of the back of the truck.

Jayda grabs me by the scruff of my jacket.

"It's only paper. You'll have a deer in a few weeks." She reassures me.

"I hope you're right." I stare out the back of the truck as the targets flutter to the ground.

2

"EWW."

I grimace at photos of a gutted deer. I'm under my covers with a flashlight reading a hunting magazine on how to dress a deer. Dressing a deer does not mean taking it out on a date. It means removing all the insides — the not-so-fun part of hunting that's necessary if we want to eat.

I've been reading all about hunting and am a little surprised by what I will have to do! Two weekends ago, after I made my five shots within a two-inch grouping using my mom's Winchester, I've been reading nonstop. During all my shooting practice, this is something we didn't discuss.

What happens to a deer after it is shot.

Somehow in my brain, I had figured out that

hunting involves practicing shooting, wearing cool camouflage clothes, walking into the wilderness and shooting a deer.

Then we'd bring it home, fry up some meat and freeze the rest.

I never accounted for the fact that someone has to take the meat off the deer.

This is called butchering, something everyone has forgotten to describe.

Hunting is nothing like grocery shopping. You don't walk down an aisle and find a cooler full of tidy white plastic-wrapped Styrofoam trays of meat.

No. Hunting is finding your food walking in the forest, stalking it, shooting it, gutting it and taking all the meat off the animal piece by piece.

I never thought about what happens between when that animal is walking around the forest and when it lands on the end of my fork.

I've been studying deer anatomy, how and where to shoot. I am excited to go hunting, but I have mixed feelings about killing an animal because I do love animals.

You have to wait to shoot until the deer is broadside,

meaning its side is turned toward you. There is a small area about the size of a grapefruit right behind the front leg where you aim. That is the lung and heart spot. You want to make the best shot possible so the animal dies right away and doesn't suffer.

Navajo and Musqua are lying next to me under the blankets. I stroke their soft fur. The thought of killing an animal makes me sad, but I understand that is our food. I love the taste of deer steak and sausages served with my kohkom's bannock.

I pet my dogs and think long and hard about this new information. I remind myself that deer are nice, but they are food and have been a part of our diet for thousands of years.

Kohkom says, "The Creator blessed us with animals to sustain us. We give thanks for them giving their lives, so we continue ours. In exchange, we take care of the land they live on, keeping the water and the air that they need to live clean. It's a circle of life."

Lying under the blankets with my dogs, hunting magazines spread around us, I decide I can do this.

I can love animals, care for them and the

environment, yet be at peace knowing I carry on traditions thousands of years old when I hunt food for my family and me. Hunting is a gift.

Usually, Moshôm and Kohkom would take me on my first hunting trip, but they've both been sick over the past couple of weeks. Next in line to take me are my parents, but Mom is working overtime, and Dad's crew is working on two large houses with short deadlines, so he says he might be out for the season.

So, Uncle Bobby and my brother Vince have offered to take me on my first deer hunt!

Vince says he got tired of swinging a hammer, and he's now at university studying to become a teacher. I don't get to see him much, so when he offered to take me hunting, I got very excited. I love spending time with him.

Navajo and Musqua lie with me as I read everything there is to know about hunting. My dad's hunting magazines say that some hunters take dogs with them. When I ask if our dogs can come with us, Uncle Bobby says no, they are pets, not trained hunting dogs, and that they would only scare the deer away.

Besides, he says you only take dogs duck hunting, to retrieve the birds.

But Navajo and Musqua are more than pets! So I've decided to train them for hunting geese and ducks.

The next day, I jump out of bed, waking Rheana with the loud *THUMP* my feet make on the floor next to her head.

"Bigfoot, could you be quieter?" she mumbles from beneath her blankets.

"Come on, boys!" I call to my dogs.

SCRATCH SCREECH BAM!

They make their way down the ramp I built for them this summer. My three-story doghouse, Caninetopia, didn't quite work as planned. It came crashing down the week after I finished it. Luckily, my dogs were not in it at the time. But I managed to salvage the slide.

And one night, after nearly breaking my back lifting my dogs into my top bunk, I had a brilliant idea. I used the salvaged slide to build a Bed-o-Matic Doggie Ramp.

My dogs can now come and go from my bunk as they please!

Mom hates the idea. She doesn't think they should be indoors at all, let alone sleeping in my bed.

But my dogs love it!

"Come on, buddies." I open the bedroom door, hunting magazines tucked under my arm.

"Shut it, Maggie!" Rheana yells, rolling over in her bed.

"You shut it . . ." I yell back. As I enter the hallway, I feel Mom's eyes on me.

"You shouldn't sleep your life away, you wonderful sister you," I correct myself, as I close the bedroom door softly.

"Morning, Mom," I say, squeezing past her into the kitchen with my dogs.

"You know I hate them in the house, Maggie."

"But they keep me warm."

"They stink and should be outside."

"So does Dez and we haven't made him sleep outside!"

"Pest!" he shouts.

"Jer . . ." I'm cut off as I open the door. Dad is staring down his nose at me, holding a paintbrush in his hand, waiting for me to finish my sentence. "Geeeronimo."

I take a bite of muffin. "Morning, Dad."

Shuffling past him, I walk into the garage, feeding pieces of muffin to Navajo and Musqua on the way.

I think my uncle is wrong. I'm sure I could train my dogs to come hunting. Clenching the muffin between my teeth, I put down my magazines and rummage through the garage. I empty boxes, search through piles of odds and ends on shelves and dump out several bags. I find old hockey trophies and team pictures of my dad with a horrible mullet. He was the team captain and still plays on a recreation team with my uncles and cousins. They call themselves the Moose Knuckles.

I yank on a heavy bag and pull as hard as I can, and everything spills out.

It's a bag full of medals. There are sporting medals from my mom. She did track and played volleyball for many years. She even went to the provincials in high school. She has a town record for the farthest shot put in the under-eighteen category.

I find wrestling trophies from my cousin Jayda and Uncle Bobby.

I pick them up one by one and place them back in the box. I move on to the next box full of old hunting gear and quickly shut that one up. It stinks! But Navajo is jumping at it. It must smell good to him.

"No." I shake my finger at him and continue to search through boxes and bags.

"AHA!"

I hold up an old squeaky toy that used to be a duck. Its wings have been torn off, and most of the fuzz that covered it has been chewed up. It used to have a squeaky ball inside it, until Navajo swallowed it. Mom got upset at him and threw the mangy old duck in a box. He'd squeak a bit whenever he tried to bark for the rest of the day. It was funny. I wanted to take him to the vet, but Mom and Dad said not to worry because he was breathing fine and whatever goes in must come out.

Sure enough, he stopped squeaking, and the next day while I was scooping up their messes in our backyard, there was the small round squeaker.

I swallow the last bite of my muffin and bounce out of the garage, my dogs chasing me. They jump up at the mangled, wingless duck I hold above my head.

"Settle down!" I walk to the middle of the yard. "SIT!"

Navajo sits down right away, tail wagging, staring at me.

Musqua tilts his head to the side, takes a poop, then starts chasing his tail.

"Nice timing, dog," I complain as I retrieve a shovel from the shed to clean up his mess. Scooping it into the metal poop bin, I return to our training session.

Navajo is still sitting quietly, wagging his tail.

"Sit!" I shout at Musqua. He's chasing a moth through Mom's pumpkin patch.

"Musqua. Sit." I shake the duck where I want him to sit.

Navajo stares at the duck in my hands, and his tail wags faster.

I point firmly at the ground. Musqua stops chasing the moth, but he refuses to sit.

"MUSQUA!"

He walks to me, tilts his head and stares. Placing the duck in my mouth, I push down on Musqua's behind. Navajo trots over and lies on his back beside him.

I pat Musqua on the head.

"'ood dog," I mumble through the duck in my mouth. "'ee, oft outh."

Musqua continues to sit obediently. I pull the duck from my mouth. "See. Soft mouth." I shake the duck in front of him, then gently close my lips around the duck again. "'ee?"

Suddenly Navajo jumps up, knocks me over and snatches the duck from my mouth.

I sit up and reach for the duck, but Musqua starts barking and jumps over me, knocking me back down.

"No! SIT!" I yell, struggling to get up. Musqua is chasing after Navajo and the mangled duck.

"STOP!"

Musqua catches up to him, and they each have an end of the duck in their mouths. They are shaking their heads in a tug-o-war over it. I jump between them and try to wrestle it from them.

"Having problems, Maggie?" Dad calls from the porch.

"Just a few."

"*Pônôtamok!*" Dad yells in Michif at the dogs to stop.

Both dogs freeze in their tracks. The duck drops from their mouths.

"*Api.*" He commands them to sit, and they obey.

I stare at them, then back at Dad.

"You're welcome," he says.

"*Chaaa*. Doesn't help if they don't listen to me." I shake my finger at them. "Bad dogs."

"What you trying to do?" Dad asks. He picks up the mangled duck and throws it across the yard. The dogs chase it.

"I'm training them to go hunting." I pick up the hunting magazines.

"HA!" Dad snorts. "Those two are lucky they know their names!"

"Dad!"

"Just saying. Cute dogs, but not the brightest crayons in the box." He ruffles my hair. "Sorry, my girl, but if you take these two hunting, you're gonna take a dip in the sloughs if you shoot a duck over the water."

Laughing, he walks into the house.

I lie on the ground with my magazines, and the dogs lie next to me. I lean on Musqua's chubby belly. It's fluffy and soft like a giant pillow. I read articles on how to unscent your hunting clothes, how to use trail cameras and tree stands, when to rattle horns to bring bucks in, when to use doe pee —

EWWWW!

I quickly sit up and read that article in detail because if my brother or uncle believe I'm going to wear doe pee like perfume to attract bucks, they are barking up the wrong tree. That is SOOOOO not going to happen!

But I am happy to report that this is not at all what the article is about. The makers of this authentic doe urine claim that if you buy their product and use the doe urine in the area you are hunting, it will attract the biggest bucks! I'm still not sure how this attracts anything, because if I smell pee, I'm going to head in the opposite direction.

Hunting tips are weird.

Bucks are male deer and have antlers. The older they are, the bigger the antlers, and hunters use some kind of point system that I don't understand. So I go inside to ask Dad about it.

"Don't worry about that. We are not trophy hunters. We are meat hunters." He rubs his belly. "We fill our freezer, and if we happen to get horns, that's just a bonus."

"Hmmm. Okay." I continue reading.

Female deer are called does, and fawns are the young deer we don't hunt. Then there is something called "rut," which has something to do with does being "in heat." I turn back to ask my dad about this, too.

He looks at me over the top of the mystery book he's reading and whispers, "Go ask your mom."

I find Mom in the kitchen, baking muffins.

"Mom, what happens when a doe is in heat? And why do bucks like the smell of their pee? That is so gross!"

"BAW HAW HAW!" she laughs so loudly her shoulders shake, and she slops some of the muffin batter onto the counter.

I stand there holding the hunting magazine open to the article "Does: Behaviors they exhibit when looking for love."

She looks back and forth between the article and me.

"Let me guess. Your dad told you to come ask me."

I nod. She leans in close.

"You know where babies come from, right?"

I feel my face turn red.

Oh, no! Not this talk again. I begin to slowly back out of the kitchen.

She continues, "When a mommy deer and a daddy deer really, really like one another —"

"I get it, Mom!"

Slamming the magazine shut, I spin on my heel in hopes of reaching my bedroom before she says anything else.

"Maggie. It's okay. It's a natural thing. It's the beautiful circle of life . . ."

Too late!

She's starting her awkward talk.

"YEP! Got it, Mom! Having babies is natural."

Running down the hall to my room, I hear my dad laughing from the living room.

This is the weird part of having a nurse as a mom. She explains everything in vivid detail and believes the more we know as kids, the less we will ask our friends or search the internet for answers. She says truth is better than lies or exaggerations. The truth is, her stories and pictures from her nursing textbooks mostly creep us out, or make us too shy to ask about anything else.

Having a nurse for a mom is great if you get hurt, but my advice is, if you have questions, don't ask!

3

ONE MAGAZINE ARTICLE SAID YOU should smell like the earth, so I gathered dirt from Mom's garden and leaves from the yard and stuffed them into a pail with my new camouflage clothes that Dad bought me.

But then in another magazine, it said to "smoke" your hunting gear with cedar and spruce boughs.

I figure the best solution is to leave them buried in dirt for a week, then hold them over a smokey fire — a smoke bath! — the day before hunting.

The morning before my big day, I jump out of bed.

"Musqua! Navajo!" They come tumbling down the doggie ramp.

SCRITCH SCRATCH BOOM.

WOOF WOOF!

They are loud in the morning.

Navajo starts to lick Rheana's sleepy face.

"Ewwww!" She pulls her blanket over her head. "Get them out of here!"

"They're just telling you how much they love you."

"They're disgusting!" She rolls over.

"Dogs have the cleanest mouths in the world."

"They lick their own butts!" She tucks herself more tightly into her blankets.

"Come on, my babies. We don't need her negativity." We head out of the room.

"Your babies are butt-lickers!" she screams.

"True! They just licked your face!" I yell, shutting the door.

Navajo, Musqua and I head to the garage. I pull the lid off the pail and dig in the dirt for my hunting clothes. I shake off the leaves, dirt and twigs. I hold them next to my face and breathe in.

SNNIIIFFFFF.

"Yep. Smells like earth." I rub the dirt from my nose and shake the leaves from the clothes. "Yuck!"

I flick off a couple of earthworms crawling from a pocket.

"Now to make a fire," I tell the dogs.

I dig out the small hibachi barbecue from the back of the garage. We use it when we go fishing. I gather twigs, sticks, leaves and paper and pile it all in front of the garage.

Lifting the top of the barbecue, I start building a little tepee from twigs and sticks above the crumpled-up paper like my dad does when we have firepits.

Grabbing Mom's garden shears, I walk to the front yard and snip off some cedar boughs, then a few spruce branches.

Before I light the fire, I flip open the magazine article that explains how to create a smoke bath. The photo shows a metal clothing rack placed above the smoke, so the clothes are a safe distance from the heat.

I find a roll of the chicken wire Mom uses in her garden and cut a large piece.

This is going to be awesome! Once I have the fire going, I'll put the wire around the hibachi to make a smoke tunnel.

The article says to use lots of tinder to cause smoke but not big flames. I think leaves will work. Pulling the barbecue lighter from my back pocket, I lean close to the little twig tepee I built in the middle of the hibachi. I flick the starter, taking a couple of tries before a small flame shoots out its tip.

I move the flame close to the dry leaves, and sparks fly.

Suddenly, *SWOOSH*, the fire takes.

Navajo and Musqua jump away from the flames.

"It's okay, guys. I know what I'm doing," I tell them.

I quickly toss more sticks and leaves on top. The flames start to dance higher, so I throw on the cedar boughs.

The fire disappears.

"Oh. Shoot." I stand back, thinking I'll have to start all over again. But I hear crackling from the barbecue, and a small puff of heavy gray smoke rises from the cedar boughs.

Leaning in close, I do what my dad does when a fire starts to go out. I blow on it gently.

He explained that fire breathes just like us. It needs

oxygen, so if you breathe on it, you help it grow.

I blow onto the embers, and they get brighter. Smoke fills my eyes, and they start tearing up. I close my eyes and blow a couple more times before backing away.

There is now a LOT of smoke rising from the small hibachi. I set the rest of the cedar and spruce boughs on top, and smoke spreads down the driveway, filling our entire yard!

Rolling the chicken wire around the hibachi, I create my smoke tunnel and hang my hunting clothes around the wire. I continue until the barbecue is no longer visible, and the smoke has nowhere to go but into my clothes.

"Woohoo! I built a smoke chamber!" I dance around my invention, surprised that it worked.

I decide to turn my clothes over every ten minutes to get a nice even smoke.

Then I notice the thick smoke is turning blue, and the flames start to rise.

ACCCHH HAAACKK.

I start to cough. I can barely see through the smoke.

"What on earth!" I hear from behind me. Dad grabs my chicken-wire smoke tunnel and throws it to the ground. A few of my clothes are on fire, and he stomps on the flames.

Meanwhile, Mom runs for the garden hose. Before she sprays my nicely smoked hunting clothes, I grab them from the ground. They are a little warm.

SPPPLLLAAASSSHHH.

SPPPLLOOOSSHHHHSIZZZZLLLLEEEE.

She sprays the hibachi. The fire dies with a slight crackle, and the last bit of smoke slowly rises.

"What in the world are you doing?" My parents stand in the driveway staring at me as I clutch my singed clothing.

"It was a smoke tunnel. For my hunting clothes."

"It was a fire tunnel!" Mom turns off the hose.

"The magazine said to smell earthy, and it's best if you take a smoke bath!"

"Well, you certainly accomplished that!" Dad laughs as he cleans up my mess.

After we finish cleaning up the yard, I go into my room to change into my cool, perfectly smoked camouflage hunting gear.

"Perfecto!" I nod at my reflection in the mirror. Strategically hiding a few burn marks, I walk into the kitchen.

Mom pulls her famous chocolate chip muffins out of the oven while Dez sits at the table.

He squints and leans back. "What is that smell?"

"I had a smoke bath."

"Better take a real bath, 'cause girl, that's rank!" Picking up his bowl, Dez leaves the kitchen.

"What's going on, Maggie Lou?" Mom asks. "I thought you were going to wait to go hunting with your dad and me."

"Oh, yeah. About that. You guys can't go until the last couple of days, so Vince and Uncle Bobby will take me tomorrow on opening day."

Mom throws her head back, laughing her loud cackle.

"Bushwalker?!" She laughs even harder. "Bushwalker is gonna take you out? Well, wear good shoes, warm clothes and be ready. You're gonna see lots of land." She messes up my hair again as she walks past me.

"Why?" I ask.

"Your brother Vincent is a Sagittarius who enjoys long walks in the forest." She shakes her head. "Once he went out to get your kohkom some ducks. He used a whole box of shells and only wounded one. We don't call him Bushwalker for no reason, my girl."

My mom grabs her coffee and leaves the kitchen, still giggling.

***

Four a.m. beeps on my clock, and I leap down from the top bunk.

BAM!

Rheana groans and turns over. "What is WRONG with you?"

"Shhh." In the dark, I feel my way to our closet and pull out a giant black garbage bag. I sealed my hunting clothes in it so they wouldn't lose their smokey odor.

I pull out items one at a time and start to get dressed.

"BLECCCH! Oh, my goodness, what is that

smell! Did you just barbecue roadkill?"

I am so excited this morning, I'm not even bothered by her comments.

"I'm going to sack me a deer today, Rheana, while you waste your life away in this bed," I announce, pretending to shoot an invisible rifle.

"BAM! BAM! BAM!"

"Oh, my gosh, Maggie Lou. It's BAG a deer. Now go away. You smell BAD." Rheana flips over in the bottom bunk.

I walk proudly into the kitchen in my smoke-bathed clothes and hunting boots.

Bushwalker and Uncle Bobby are already in the kitchen, drinking coffee.

"Whoa." Bushwalker shakes his head away from me. "Where's the fire?"

"What is that smell?" Uncle Bobby asks.

"The hunting magazine said to take a smoke bath," I say.

"Wow. Let's hope the deer like smoked oysters!"

"You truly are something else, Maggie Lou!" Bushwalker says as he places bread in the toaster. "Oh, yeah, did you hear the rumor going around about butter?" He breaks out in laughter. "Never mind, let's not spread it!"

Uncle Bobby shakes his head and hands me a small cup. "A good ol' cup of joe to wake you up!"

"But I'm only thirteen!"

"Yeah, but you're a hunter today. Drink up."

Feeling two inches taller, I hold my head high and take a big swig. The coffee sprays right back out of my mouth and through my nose, and lands all over the counter and Uncle Bobby's sleeve.

"BLECCCH! YUK!" I cough and sputter. "It tastes like hot garbage!"

Uncle Bobby and Bushwalker stand there laughing.

This adventure is starting off with a bitter taste. And maybe, I admit to myself, a bad smell.

4

LIGHT SNOW IS BEGINNING TO FALL. The three of us pile into Uncle Bobby's truck. I sit bundled up in the back seat, bouncing around as we drive across the fields. They crack all the windows because the guys say the smokey-oyster smell of my clothing is turning their stomachs. It gets a little chilly in the back seat, but I don't care. I'm so excited this day has finally come!

Uncle parks the truck alongside a bluff of trees. The two of them sit and stare out into the darkness. I sit up and stare, too. But I don't know what they're looking at. I can't see anything because it's too dark.

Whispering, Uncle Bobby and Bushwalker plan who's going to go where. Who's going to do what, and how this hunt will go down. Uncle

Bobby pushes a bottle of Scent Killer in front of Bushwalker, but he whispers, "I have enough on." They argue for a bit, and we get out of the truck. Then they turn to me and spray my front, back and bottom of my boots.

Scent Killer is supposed to get rid of any smell. But I still smell like smoked oysters.

"Okay, Smokey Oakley," Bushwalker says. "Let's get this show on the road."

We start walking.

And walk some more.

We walk and walk. We tiptoe. Then we creep along slowly. Uncle Bobby puts his hand up and we stop. Then we walk some more. We walk through the bushes. We walk around the bushes. We walk up hills and down hills. Uncle points at deer tracks on the ground. Bushwalker nods and then points his lips in a different direction. Then we creep along some more.

I try not to talk much, but I get shushed even for whispering.

As far as I can tell, hunting is a lot of walking and no talking. This is getting hard.

My mom was right. All I will see is a lot of land. My legs are getting tired.

I am bored. I want to quit.

Finally, as we approach a large bluff of poplars, Uncle and Bushwalker point and grunt in some secret hunter language.

I shake my head that I don't understand.

"Stay here," Bushwalker whispers. "Sit down. Don't move. Face this way. If a deer comes, you know what to do. We are going to push bush."

I am equal parts scared and excited. So I crouch down in the frosty grass, going over all the lessons I've been reading in my hunting magazines and imagining the anatomy of the deer and repeating, "Gonna sack me a bag ... deer me a sack ... I'm going to get a deer!"

After I walked and walked, now I get to sit and sit. I sit for what feels like a long time. Then I sit some more, and when that is done, I sit a little longer.

My legs are getting sore. I shift from crouching to kneeling, to sitting cross-legged and then stretching my legs straight in front of me.

My arms start to get tired, and I set my rifle

down. As I look around, the sun is rising in the east, and I see lots of trees and fields around me, but no deer. I start to braid the grass surrounding me.

What's the big deal about hunting? All I've done is walk and sit! I could have stayed in my warm bed.

And suddenly . . .

CRUNCH. CRUNCH. CRUNCH.

I slowly turn my head to the right and see a small buck eating grass. He is taller than me and has two points on each of his antlers.

My heart skips a beat, then starts pounding quickly in my chest. I mentally race through all the lessons I've been taught, all the articles I've read, but all I can remember are the lines of my favorite song: "Never gonna give you up . . . never gonna let you down . . ."

I close my eyes. *Focus, Maggie Lou! Focus!*

Then I remember that my rifle is down in the grass beside me.

CRUNCH. CRUNCH. CRUNCH.

I look at my rifle. I look at the deer. I take a deep breath and slowly lean toward my rifle.

CRUNCH. CRUNCH. CRUNCH.

Then suddenly, off in the distance . . .

BANG! BANG! BANG!

From far away, I hear three shots ring out. The deer looks up.

BANG BANG.

The buck takes off.

A minute or so later, I hear another three shots.

BANG BANG BANG.

WOW! We are going to have lots of deer. I think about juicy steaks for supper and the family and friends we'll share all this food with. I'm so proud of Bushwalker and Uncle Bobby.

Later, we sit in the truck and eat the lunch my mom packed: cheese sandwiches for me and ham for the boys, chips, carrot sticks and apple juice. Uncle Bobby and Bushwalker are arguing over who's to blame for missing the buck and the two does they sneaked up on. Bushwalker said Uncle Bobby scared them off with his loud breathing and that he hadn't applied enough Scent Killer. Uncle Bobby yells between bites that it doesn't matter because Bushwalker couldn't hit the broad side of a barn if it were gift-wrapped and placed in front of him.

This arguing goes on forever as I eat my lunch quietly in the back seat. I decide this isn't the best time to mention the buck that was a few feet from me while I was busy braiding dead grass.

I miss my bed. All I've learned about hunting so far is that you walk and walk, sit and sit, then wait. And at the end, you quietly chew on dry carrots in the back of the truck so you don't disturb the men arguing in the front seat.

I bounce in the back seat as Uncle Bobby drives around the bumpy farm fields. I hang on to the door handle so I don't slip out of the seatbelt and crash onto the floor. We cross endless back roads searching for the deer's evening grazing spot. Bushwalker scans for deer using binoculars. We pass plenty of other hunters, a parade of camouflage and bright orange toques.

The whole time, my uncle and brother argue over who was at fault for missing the deer and how they will get one this evening. I even have a little nap while they drive around arguing and telling stories I've already heard a million times. Like when Uncle Bobby shot the back leg off a deer, and that three-legged deer still got away. Or the time Bushwalker stalked a giant buck for three hours, and then when he was eighty yards from it he went to pull the trigger and was met with a *click-click* because he forgot to load his gun.

All stories I've heard again and again at family gatherings.

Uncle Bobby parks on another dirt road, and once again we walk and walk. We walk quietly. Then we walk slowly. They nod and grunt along the way. Uncle signals something in their mysterious hunter sign language and leaves us. Bushwalker nods and motions for me to follow him.

As we continue walking down the tree line, I finally understand how my brother got the name Bushwalker. No wonder Mom laughed so hard when I told her Bushwalker was taking me hunting. She was right. This is turning into one of the longest days of my life, and I think I'm getting a blister.

My brother signals for me to lean in and he whispers, "Why did the deer get braces?" I pull away. He draws me in close again, "Because he had buck teeth." He releases my shoulders, laughing silently and then motions for me to sit quietly. I follow his instructions while he continues to walk down the tree line.

I sit and sit. Then I sit some more. I will be careful not to put my rifle down or braid grass this time.

I look up at the sky and start to imagine animals in the shape of clouds. A large fluffy cloud slowly breaks into two. One piece looks like a small monkey and the other like a blue whale with a wide-open mouth. But the clouds shift, and the monkey cloud starts to ride on the whale's back.

The whale and monkey disappear.

The sun is going down. I don't like this.

I am all alone on this tree line for what feels like an eternity. I twirl and chew the ends of my hair. I close my eyes and pretend Musqua and Navajo are on either side of me wagging their fluffy tails, and I feel calm.

I don't know how long I have my eyes closed as I sit in these trees. All I'm hoping is that my uncle or brother will call out my name when suddenly …

PHWWWWWWHHT!

The wind whistles eerily through the trees, and

my eyes snap open. I look around to realize I am alone.

What if my uncle and brother forgot about me?

5

"PSST PSST PSSSSSSST!"

Slowly I get up. I look around, whispering.

But only the wind answers with a creepy whistle through the trees, and tiny snowflakes start to fall.

After a few minutes of softly calling their names and looking around, I decide to walk back to the truck. My brother marked the trail with orange tape, and I know it is a straight walk down the tree line back to the road.

So I start to walk and walk. I walk some more. It feels like I have been walking forever.

Then suddenly . . .

A large shadow emerges from the tree line.

I freeze.

CLOMP CLOMP CLOMP go its hooves.

A giant black moose stands in front of me. His enormous antlers are flat like paddles on either side of his head. They are wider than his shoulders.

I slowly back into the trees, hoping the moose will forget about me and leave, but he doesn't. He is a curious moose and saunters toward me.

CLOMP CLOMP CLOMP!

He stops to study me. Turning his huge hairy head side to side, he lets out a snort.

PLOUF!

I back up more and try to hide behind a skinny poplar tree.

Again, the moose turns his head from side to side. He studies me carefully, like a fox inspecting a henhouse. He snorts twice.

PLOUF! PLOUF!

I close my eyes. *If I can't see you, you can't see me.*

I hold my breath, and when I open my eyes the moose is still standing there.

His head is so enormous. His eyes are like two black holes that go on forever. His nose hangs off his face like Santa's belly, and when he breathes, I can see his nostrils flare.

Finally, the moose gets bored staring at me. He slowly turns and walks away on his long spindly legs.

Exhaling with a slow and quiet *phew*, I relax my shoulders.

Once the moose is out of sight, I continue to walk down the tree line toward the truck.

CRUNCH CRUNCH CRUNCH goes the light dusting of crisp snow on the ground. I carefully follow the orange tape tied to the trees.

It is getting dark, and I don't like being out here alone. I don't like this hunting business anymore.

Suddenly . . .

ARH-ARH-ARH-WOOOOOOOOO!

I hear a pack of coyotes calling out. Or maybe it's wolves? I try to recall the article I read in one of my hunting magazines but can't remember which is more dangerous. Did it say coyotes calm and wolves wary? Or was it coyote crazy and welcoming wolves?

Either way, I am not sticking around to find out. I am positive they are in the trees following me. I panic and walk faster, no longer trying to be quiet.

STOMP STOMP STOMP!

The more they howl, the faster I walk.

I scan the open field and spot a combine. It is big and green, and I remember passing it on our way down the tree line. I now know my uncle's truck isn't far away. But, with the next howl — *ARH-ARH-ARH-WOOOOOOOO!* — and the sound of what I think is branches breaking behind me, I head as fast as I can for that green John Deere combine.

Next to the combine, I unload my rifle with shaking hands, make sure the safety is on, and strap it to my back before climbing up. From the driver's seat inside the cab, I survey the dusky field and tree line, wondering where my uncle and brother are. I imagine I am a soldier on the watchtower of an ancient castle, ready to fight dragons that might emerge from the trees.

As time goes on, I begin to get mad at my uncle and brother for leaving me alone. *Great! My first hunting trip, I was almost attacked by a moose and now I could get eaten by wolves.*

I sit some more. The sun has dropped, but thankfully there is still plenty of light for me to stand guard. I lean back on the glass door and think, *All their hunting stories are made up. Maybe the meat they bring home is actually from the store.*

Suddenly I hear, "Maggie Lou, what the heck are you doing up there?" I open my eyes to see Bushwalker marching across the field. "I told you to stay put!" He sounds upset as he helps me down.

"Well, first off, *Bushwalker*, you didn't tell me anything! You grunted and nodded to me. I sat where you grunted to. Then it started getting dark. I thought you guys forgot about me. So I started to walk!"

He shakes his head and starts walking away from me.

"Then you know what happened?" I follow him. "A moose!" I tap him on the back. "Did you hear me?" I'm walking quickly to keep up with him.

He shakes his head.

"Yes, a moose found me!"

Vince turns and looks down his nose at me, irritated. "A moose?"

"Yes, a giant moose came after me! He was mad and didn't like me!"

"Well, I don't believe you." He continues walking.

"We scoured this entire bush and there were no moose."

"Then you know what happened? There was a pack of coyotes!" I struggle to keep up with his long strides. "They started howling! They didn't like me either, and they started chasing me down!"

Laughing, he reaches behind him and pulls my orange toque down over my eyes.

"A giant moose and a pack of wild coyotes! Oh, you're a laugh! We haven't seen or heard anything all evening."

I push the toque back up on top of my head, stumbling to follow behind him.

"Really bro! No lie!"

"Maggie Lou and her crazy imagination," he says as we walk.

"His eyes were like big black saucers, and he stared right into my soul!"

"Little sis with the big mouth, always full of stories."

"Whatever, Bushwalker!" I mumble behind him. "You didn't see the moose or hear the coyotes, but I did!"

We reach the truck, where Uncle Bobby sits on the hood drinking coffee.

"There she is! Prairiewalker, sister of Bushwalker!" He bursts out laughing. "You two are quite the pair!"

My brother guffaws. They unload their rifles and double-check mine before placing them in their cases and tucking them safely into the back.

"Think I'll leave Smokey and the Bandit at home tomorrow," Uncle says as he starts his truck. "Y'all are bad luck."

Sitting in the back seat with my sore feet, I think of all the hunting lessons I learned today. You walk a lot. You sit a lot. You argue. You walk some more. You tell big stories about previous hunting trips, you eat in between, and at the end you call each other names.

Yawning, I lean back into the seat and think of my new nickname. Prairiewalker, Sister of Bushwalker. I think it's funny. Better than Smokey Oakley, but I'm not sure which one will stick. With my family, you never know.

I open my eyes as we slow down in front of my house. The headlights light up the dark driveway.

My parents and siblings are unpacking grocery bags from the back of the car.

"Look at those sad faces!" Mom calls out.

"Well, if ain't Smokey Oakley, the Bandit and Cledus!" Dad points at us, laughs and carries groceries inside the house, apparently referring to some old movie I have no clue about.

Bushwalker and Uncle Bobby start to argue about who was at fault for missing that buck. The three of us slowly unpack the truck, dreading going inside to be the target of our family's comedy routine.

As the three of us lean against Bobby's truck, Kohkom and Moshôm come shuffling up the sidewalk. Kohkom is carrying fresh bannock wrapped in tea towels. I can see steam rising from it. My mouth starts to water at its delicious smell.

"Kitimâki mâcêwak!" Kohkom laughs as she climbs the stairs.

"Sad hunters," Moshôm translates for me, smiling.

"That's okay. Come eat." Kohkom opens the front door and waves us in.

We climb the stairs. Removing our boots, we

leave them on the porch and go inside to face the heckling.

"*Tân'sī*, Bushwalker!" Mom calls from the kitchen. "Cover lots of miles today?"

"Yes. And meet his sister, Prairiewalker!" Uncle Bobby grabs my shoulders, shaking them to make his point. "You should have seen these two kicking stones as they came walking back!"

My family thinks they are all comedians, and their teasing is endless, especially when you do something silly or wrong. It's our way of connecting, Kohkom says.

"My boy, how much ammo you waste today?" Kohkom jokes.

We make our way to the kitchen as Uncle and Vince continue to argue over who messed up worse today, each blaming the other.

"Well, Smokey Oakley? See anything?" Moshôm asks, winking.

I shake my head, leaning over the counter where Mom is slicing up Kohkom's bannock.

"Oh, don't lie, sis!" Bushwalker pipes up. "You saw a giant moose, thirty coyotes, and I'm sure the back of your eyelids when we found you napping!"

The room breaks out in more laughter.

"How could you sleep through that smell!" Rheana cuts in. "Please go change!"

"I'm thinking that's what scared all the deer away today. They thought smoked oysters were on the menu and they're not seafood fans!" Bobby snorts.

"Hey! Don't start blaming the youngest for your bad hunting skills!" Dad laughs and smacks Uncle Bobby on the back.

"Okay. Okay. Just come eat." Kohkom carries the plate of fresh bannock to the table.

"My boy, grab the meat from the fridge," Mom calls out.

"Sure thing."

We all take a seat and start passing around plates and knives. Moshôm butters his bannock.

"Well, if it weren't for your kohkom's bannock, we'd all starve," he jokes as he takes a bite.

Vince carries a large plate to the table.

"Very funny!" he says as he puts down the plate.

A silver platter decorated with pieces of shiny pink slabs piled on top of one another sits in the middle as Mom ceremoniously removes the plastic wrap.

She's used our Christmas reindeer cookie cutter to slice up bologna and placed Vince's orange deer tag on top of the cute bologna deer in the shape of a bow.

We all burst out laughing.

"I told you, my girl." Mom messes up my hair. "Your brother can only hunt bologna sandwiches."

Biting into my bologna-deer sandwich, I lean back and listen to my family laughing and joking together.

"Poor little Prairiewalker here didn't even see any deer today!" Uncle Bobby announces.

I smile, thinking about the buck eating grass beside my napping spot. I take another bite of my sandwich and slowly nod at my uncle.

"You'll have better luck next time, Maggie," Jayda says through a mouthful of bannock. "When you come out with a real hunter." She flexes her biceps. "Next weekend, my girl. You and me." She leans across to high-five me. "We won't waste any brass. We'll drop 150 pounds and be home by noon."

"Deal!" I smack her hand.

"A hundred and fifty? That's all?" Uncle Bobby responds.

"Are we betting on the biggest haul this fall?" Jayda looks around the table.

"A buck a pound," Vince says.

"Bushwalker, you're a student now. You can't afford that!" Dad jokes.

"I can't afford not to!" Bushwalker extends his hand to the center of the table. "Gotta get rid of that name!"

Mom laughs. "Oh, son." She shakes his hand and all the hunters start shaking hands in agreement to the buck-a-pound bet. "Once named, always named."

Mom winks at me. "Right, Prairiewalker?"

I giggle because it's true. Once our family has given you a nickname, there's no going back! Unless you're special like me, and you get two!

It's our family tradition.

AUTHOR'S NOTE

THANK YOU SO MUCH FOR reading *Maggie Lou, Firefox*. This fiery character is very near and dear to me on so many levels, as I come from a long line of strong women. I wanted to share my vibrant Métis culture, our Michif language and our sense of humor with you. It was also my desire to provide a courageous girl hero for other young people who love to dance across the lines that divide us.

I grew up knowing I could be anything I wanted. My parents always encouraged me to be brave and, to quote my mom, "never be afraid to fail." (This is the same mom who yelled, "Don't you dare bleed on my seats!" as she drove me — yet again — to the hospital for stitches.)

Maggie Lou is a vivid picture of some of my experiences growing up as a young girl in a colorful Métis family in Saskatchewan. All her stories are genuine but may have been changed or embellished to benefit the reader and the story. I also slipped in a few of my daughters' exploits, as the apples didn't fall far from the tree. They are just as fiery and mischievous as their mother. All the characters in Maggie's family reflect someone special in my life, and I hope you enjoyed meeting them.

I pray these stories open a small window into our Métis family, leave you laughing and inspire you to voyage through life courageously. Do not go through life being a small version of yourself. Be fierce, be strong and unapologetically your beautiful and intelligent self!

Keep on dreaming.

Arnolda

P.S. Please write to me or follow my future projects on arnoldadufourbowes.com.

GLOSSARY

This book includes a number of Indigenous slang and Northern Michif words. Michif is a combination of Cree and French and is one of the languages spoken by the Métis people. The Michif language is diverse, and the dialect can vary, depending on the area one is from.

With thanks to Vince Ahenakew for his translation and assistance. For more about the Michif language, please download the Northern-Michif-To-Go app or consult *Nêhiyawêwin Masiniahikkan: Michif**/ *Cree Dictionary* and *Nêhiyawêwin Mitâtaht: Michif Ahci Cree Combo* by Vince Ahenakew: gdins.org/product/michifcree-dictionaryandgrammarguide/.

Api – sit
Âstam – come here
Awas – go away
Chaa – expression of disbelief (Indigenous slang)
Hâ mâka – hurry up
Iskotêw Mahkîsîs – Firefox

Kitakahkowîpin'kân – well done
Kitimâki mâcêwak – sad hunters
Kohkom – grandmother
Kwayes kotôtîn – you did well
Marrsî – thank you
Moshôm – grandfather
Pônôtamok – stop
Pôn'wêwita – be quiet
Rabbit Dance – a traditional Métis dance done to a fiddle tune in partners, following a figure eight
Scrime – expression of exasperation (Indigenous slang)
Skoden – let's go then (Indigenous slang)
Stoodis – let's do this (Indigenous slang)
Tân'si – hello

ARNOLDA DUFOUR BOWES is a a Métis writer with family ties to Sakitawak (Île à la Crosse) and George Gordon First Nation, and she has lived around the world, from New Zealand to Saudi Arabia. She has worked in vocations from nursing to construction and loves new adventures — everything from skydiving to surfing. She is the author of *20.12 m: A Short Story Collection of a Life Lived as a Road Allowance Métis*, which won the Danuta Gleed Literary Award and the High Plains Book Award.

Arnolda lives with her husband, three children and two dogs in Dalmeny, Saskatchewan.